P9-CQW-214

The
BIG SPLASH

The
BIG S

By JACK D. FERRAIOLO

Amulet Books
New York

Library of Congress Cataloging-in-Publication Data

Ferraiolo, Jack D.
The big splash / by Jack D. Ferraiolo.
p. cm.
Summary: Matt Stevens, an average middle schooler with a glib tongue and a knack for solving crimes, uncovers a mystery while working with "the organization," a mafia-like syndicate run by seventh-grader Vincent "Mr. Biggs" Biggio, specializing in forged hall passes, test-copying rings, black market candy selling, and taking out hits with water guns.
ISBN 978-0-8109-7067-0 (harry n. abrams : alk. paper)
[1. Junior high schools—Fiction. 2. Schools—Fiction. 3. Mystery and detective stories. 4. Humorous stories.] I. Title.
PZ7.F3637Bi 2008
[Fic]—dc22
200704

Book design by Chad W. Beckerman

Printed and bound in U.S.A.
10 9 8 7 6 5 4 3 2 1

To Teryse . . . for
everything . . .
-J.F.

SOMEONE TOOK DOWN NIKKI FINGERS, THE MOST FEARED SQUIRT-GUN ASSASSIN AT FRANKLIN MIDDLE SCHOOL! MATT STEVENS IS ON THE CASE!

THE SUSPECTS:

Vincent "Vinny Biggs" Biggio, the boss
Kevin Carling, the right-hand man
Liz Carling, the protective sister
Joey "the Hyena" Renoni, the hit man
Melanie Kondo, the scorned girl
Jenny Finnegan, the resentful sister
Jimmy MacGregor, the reporter longing for a big story
Or one of a hundred kids who had a reason to hate Nikki . . .

He approached me as I made my way into the caf for lunch. He was small and wiry, with a face that would've been more at home on a rodent. His jaw moved slowly and with great purpose as it worked over a piece of fruit gum, the kind that gave off a sickeningly sweet smell but lost its flavor after three chews. His name was Joey Renoni, a.k.a. "the Hyena," and I knew who he worked for.

"Stevens," he spit out, "Mr. Biggs wants to see you, hehehe." A short, high-pitched giggle ended his sentence, justifying his nickname. He scanned the crowd constantly as we walked, his head swiveling back and forth in a herky-jerky motion, like a lawn sprinkler with the hiccups.

"Tell him to call my secretary and make an appointment," I replied.

"It wasn't a request, hehehe."

"Everything is a request. Ever heard of freedom of choice?"

He stopped walking. "All right, smart guy . . . here's your choice: You can *choose* to talk to Biggs or you can *choose* to get popped, hehehe."

He sneered at me, revealing teeth that had enjoyed one Jawbreaker too many. His right hand went to the side pocket of his cargo pants. There was a lump there the approximate size and shape of a squirt gun. Smart guy that I was, I got the message. He raised an eyebrow and waited for my response.

"You know, I've been wanting to talk to Vinny for a while," I said. "Today's as good a day as any."

"Good choice, hehehe." He started walking again. I followed.

The place was packed with seventh graders, not a huge stretch for a middle-school cafeteria at lunchtime. It was spaghetti day, so the air was thick with the smell of government-supplied tomato sauce. Joey walked in front of me, cutting a swath through the crowd. Nobody wanted to accidentally bump into him because they would "accidentally" get bumped back, only ten times harder. Joey wasn't a big kid, but he was crazy, and crazy trumped size. Size could be negotiated with. Nobody knows what to do with crazy.

Vinny Biggs's table was in the back right corner of the caf, strategically chosen for its view of the entire room. Vinny sat with his back to the wall, so that only ghosts had a shot of sneaking up on him. As Joey and I approached, two hulking eighth graders moved to block our path. Joey gave them a barely perceptible nod. Before I could protest, they lifted me off the ground and guided me toward the wall, as gently as two grizzlies playing with a bunny rabbit.

"Routine weapons check," one of them rumbled.

"Just doing our job," said the other.

"Ooof, ow . . . ," I replied.

They did everything but buy me lunch. When they didn't find any squirt guns on me, they let me through. One of them even helped me sit down, hard.

Vinny was using his meaty hands to delicately eat a

salad too green and fresh to have been gotten from the cafeteria. Sitting to his left was his right-hand man, Kevin Carling, eating potato chips one at a time, wiping the salt from his fingers after each one. They both wore freshly pressed dress shirts and khakis, making them look like businessmen that someone had left in the dryer too long. Kevin and I had been best friends back in Ellie. Now the big jerk was just another one of Vinny's lackeys.

I crossed my arms and waited for Vinny to acknowledge my arrival, but he kept right on eating his salad. I checked my watch. My lunch period was slipping away.

I cleared my throat too loud and too long to be authentic. "Ahem."

"Hey, Matt," Kevin said, then shot me a smile I didn't return. Vinny didn't look up.

"That's doing wonders for your figure," I said, nodding toward Vinny's salad.

Vinny smiled in spite of himself. He looked up at me. "A fat joke? Matthew, I expected better of you."

"I guess getting manhandled makes me cranky."

He shrugged, then dabbed the corners of his mouth with a napkin.

"Did you call me here just to watch you eat?" I asked. "Not that it isn't fascinating."

"Not quite," he said. "Are you still for hire, or did things change over the summer?"

"I'm still a private detective, if that's what you mean."

"Excellent. I have a job for you."

I stood up in a hurry. "Thanks, but no thanks. *Not* being one of your lackeys helps me sleep at night."

"Please, sit down and hear me out first."

This wasn't a request. One of the guards helped me to my seat again.

"Your goons can keep me here to listen to your 'job offer,'" I growled, "but the chances of me taking it are slim."

"Matthew, why the hostility? I thought we got along."

"We used to get along. Now we coexist."

"Well, then let me put it to you this way: You were one of the few people who stood up for me before I attained my current position. I always felt like I should do you a favor somehow, so—"

"Whoa," I said, "the people you do favors for either

land in detention or end up getting popped. How about just a thank you and a hearty handshake?"

"How about a thank you, a hearty handshake, and twenty dollars?"

My mouth snapped shut. Twenty bucks was a lot of money. I mean, there's stuff I wouldn't do for twenty bucks, but the list was pretty short. Vinny was watching me, grinning broadly. Apparently, I wore my thoughts like makeup on a little girl: all over my face.

"Ahhh," he purred, "I knew you'd do it."

"I'm not 'doing' anything . . . yet. Twenty dollars gets my attention, not my services. What's the job?"

"Simple. There's a trinket, a good luck charm. I lent it out to someone a long time ago, and now I want it back."

"Sounds like a job for one of your goons."

"Employees, Matthew. Not goons. And yes, it would seem to be, but it isn't. This job requires more . . . finesse."

"Why not use Kevin?" I asked, nodding in his direction. "He's not as brutish as the rest of your 'employees.' I heard he's even housebroken."

"Kevin can't do this job," Vinny said, in a way that closed the subject.

I looked at Kevin. His eyes were no longer locked on my face. They had suddenly taken a strong interest in his shoes. His smile now resembled a grimace, as if he had just been hit in the stomach with a two-by-four. There was only one kid in school who could make Kevin look that way.

"Who'd you lend it to?" I asked, even though I already knew the answer.

"Nicole Finnegan."

I barked out a laugh. "Right. You expect me to go up to Nikki Fingers, only the most feared trigger-girl in school, and force her to hand over your good luck charm. You have another one *I* could borrow?"

"It isn't like that."

"Well, how is it like?"

"You know as well as I do that over the summer she decided to stop working for me. She's out . . . completely out. She wouldn't hurt a kitten."

"I'm not as cute as a kitten."

Vinny ignored me and continued. "And you wouldn't be 'forcing' her to do anything, Matthew. I doubt she even remembers she has it. And if she does remember, I doubt that she'd have any problem parting with it. I gave it to her last year. We used to joke that it gave her good luck."

"If it's her good luck charm, why would she give it up?"

"She needed it when she worked for me," he said. "She certainly doesn't need it now."

"Everybody needs good luck."

"True, but not everybody needs the same kind."

I nodded, conceding his point. "So why hire me?" I asked. "You don't need a detective. You already know who has the charm. And there must be someone in your organization with enough brains and manners to ask Nikki for something she doesn't want anymore."

"There are, but Nicole and I made a deal. She would never talk about my organization to anyone, and I would never approach her again. We both wanted a clean break."

"That doesn't really answer my question."

"Doesn't it? You're a neutral party, Matthew. You don't work for me—"

"But you would be hiring me."

"Technically, yes. But let's face it, everyone knows you would never 'work' for me, not in any way that really mattered."

"What if she refuses?"

"If she refuses, then nothing. I want my trinket back, but not that badly. I respect her way too much to try to force it from her." His gaze went distant for a moment. "In a way, it would be nice if she refused. She was the best . . . my favorite . . . and if she wants to keep the trinket as a token of what we once had, then I would be flattered." Out of the corner of my eye, I saw Joey make an ugly face, as if what Vinny said didn't sit too well. Then again, maybe I was reading too much into it; the Hyena had a lot of faces, none of them pretty. I turned my attention back to Vinny.

"Sounds easy. What's the catch?"

"No catch. You ask her for the trinket. Whether you get it back from her or not, I pay you twenty dollars. Consider it back pay for being nice to me before you had to."

It sounded plausible, but trusting Vinny Biggs was like signing your own detention slip. Twenty bucks, however, was hard to ignore, no matter what the risks were.

"What does the trinket look like?"

Vinny smiled. "It's a hula girl, holding a surfboard."

"What's the time frame?"

"The sooner the better."

"How's this afternoon?" I asked.

"Fine."

"Fine. Half now, half after the job's done," I said.

Vinny put ten dollars on the table. His smile widened. He had been holding it in his hand the entire time. He had known what I wanted before I did. I frowned, but picked up the bill and put it in my pocket before I could change my mind. He slid something else across the table. It was a hall pass with my name on it.

"So you can eat your lunch in peace," he said, "without rushing."

I picked up the pass and looked at it. It was expertly forged. My frown sunk a little lower.

The bell rang. Vinny stood up; I didn't move. "Don't question your decision, Matthew," he said, reading my mind via my face again. He walked over and put his hand on my shoulder. "A smart kid knows a good deal when it falls into his lap."

He clapped my shoulder twice, like an over-friendly politician, then walked out of the caf with his entourage trailing behind him. Joey the Hyena lingered for a moment. His eyes were full of malice. "See you around, Stevens," he said, then giggled that eerie giggle of his. "Hehehe . . ."

I sat there cursing myself for breaking one of my longest-standing rules: Don't *ever* work for Vinny Biggs, especially on deals that were too good to be true. Nothing that paid well was ever easy.

I sleepwalked through the rest of my classes that afternoon, only making a fool of myself in History. When Mr. Donnelly asked me who started the Peloponnesian War, I almost answered "Nikki Fingers."

Luckily, I had a seventh-period study hall, which gave me an opportunity to catch up with my thoughts about Nikki and Vinny's sordid past. Nicole Finnegan, a.k.a. Nikki Fingers, was a dream girl . . . the kind who caused nightmares. She was twelve, but could have easily passed for fourteen. One glimpse of her bright red hair and luminous green eyes made you freeze like a package of fish sticks, and that was all the time she needed to shoot so much water on the front of your pants, it looked like your bladder exploded. She was a big reason behind Vinny's rise to power in the middle-school underworld.

One year ago, the Franklin Middle School landscape looked a whole lot different. Small-time scams ran rampant at the Frank: kids shaken down for lunch money, stolen exams sold on the black market, that sort of thing. There was no organization to it. Everyone was out for themselves. At the time, Vincent Biggio was just a short, chubby, sixth-grade target for upper-class bullies. Each bully took his shots, but one in particular seemed to want to turn torturing Vinny into a career. Richard Dexter, or Dickie Dex as he was known, was a two-time eighth grader whose only ambition seemed to be to make the middle school need Driver's Ed. He fulfilled all the requirements of your average, run-of-the-mill bully: big, dumb, and vaguely greasy. He must have been waiting for someone like Vinny his whole life, because from day one, Dickie was all over him like hair on an old man's ear.

"Hey fatboy!" he used to call out, laughing at his own lame attempt at humor. Vinny would take it all stoically:

the laughing, the name-calling, the beatings. When Kevin and I were still friends, we were able to step in a couple of times and bail him out. We didn't do it because we were friends with Vinny; we did it because we hated bullies. Unfortunately, we couldn't be everywhere, and when we weren't around, Vinny took his lumps.

Nobody knew it at the time, but Vinny was more than just a punching bag. He was a punching bag with a plan: to take control of all illegal activities in school. He started by trafficking stolen exams. First, he recruited kids with honest faces and sticky fingers, promising them big payoffs for hot tests. He hired salespeople in each grade to peddle the goods to whoever would buy. Vinny was true to his word: Sales took off, grades went up, the money rolled in, and everyone was happy.

Next, he went into trafficking candy. He lobbied to stop the cafeteria from selling sweets, playing on the child-obesity fears of well-meaning adults. Vinny became a poster boy for the cause, saying that his weight problem was the fault of the cafeteria's menu. Almost overnight, all the junk food disappeared. The students' desire for junk food, however, didn't go anywhere. Once the attention from adults disappeared, Vinny was more than happy to feed the students' needs. He got some stickers with APPROVED printed on them, then invested in big boxes of candy from one of those wholesale clubs. Only candy "approved" by Vinny was allowed in the school, and he hired some eighth-grade muscle to make sure it stayed that way. Vinny's fortunes grew, and so did his organization.

He recruited more kids to handle the load of his expanding business. Divisions and ranks were forming, but weren't fully in place yet. Vinny offered kids a chance to get in on the ground floor. He developed a system, ways to move up the ranks by performing certain tasks or hitting certain sales goals. The details of the system were kept secret, and only kids in his crew knew how it worked. It was around this time that he approached me with an offer: join his crew as his lieutenant, his right-hand man.

He promised me money and power. I wouldn't have to work my way through the ranks; I could start out at the top, helping him mold and shape his organization. I felt like a diabetic at an ice cream buffet: I was tempted, but I knew it wouldn't be very good for me. I politely declined. Later that afternoon, Vinny made the same offer to Kevin. He jumped at the chance.

I remember being bowled over by the news, and feeling

more than a little betrayed. I confronted Kevin and asked him if he realized that "lieutenant" in this case was just a fancy word for "bully."

"No it isn't," he responded. "Vinny's going to put the bullies out of business."

"Yeah, because they're the competition, you idiot!"

"You don't know what you're talking about, Matt."

"You're right. Vinny's doing all this illegal stuff out of the goodness of his heart," I said with mock sincerity. "You're not really that naive, are you?"

Kevin sighed, then looked at me with a weird expression: his mouth pinched in a little frown; his gaze dropped and avoided my face. "There are a lot of reasons to do something, Matt. Not all of them are going to have your approval."

"What the hell does that mean?"

"I don't want to talk about it."

"Even with me? Come on, man. I'm your best friend."

He shrugged as if that didn't mean much at the moment. "Maybe you don't know me as well as you think you do," he said.

I was suddenly furious. "If you're doing something this dumb," I said, "maybe I don't know you at all."

All he did was shrug again and walk away as if our six years of friendship meant nothing. We didn't see much of each other outside of class after that. After a while, I even got pretty good at pretending it didn't bother me. Not that it mattered; Kevin was too busy with his new "job" to notice.

With Kevin's help, Vinny worked his way into forgeries: doctor's notes, hall passes, report cards, anything official. Then they went after the big money: gambling. They set up books for all the school's sports teams. It was a good plan, but it had a major flaw: A lot of kids still didn't respect Vinny, despite the fact that he now controlled every illegal activity in school. When some kids lost their bets, they refused to pay up. They still thought of Vinny as a pudgy little punching bag, and no amount of money or crimes committed was going to change that. Vinny's organization was missing one crucial ingredient: Nicole Finnegan.

I remember seeing Nicole on my first day of sixth, before she went to work for Vinny. She was a cute but unremarkable little red-haired girl. When I introduced myself, she said hello, then politely shook my hand. It was like shoving my hand into a snowbank. She seemed completely in control of herself, in a way that most girls her age weren't. I remember thinking that Nicole was going to leave a lot of broken hearts in her wake. I had no idea how right I was.

It started with Jimmy Forrester, a seventh-grade hood as small-time as they come. Jimmy used to use Vinny as his own personal ATM, shaking him down whenever he needed a little extra dough. The last time Jimmy tried this, Vinny suggested that he go jump off a bridge. At first, Jimmy laughed—he thought it was a practical joke set up by his friends. When he realized Vinny was serious, he laughed again, then blackened Vinny's eye. He shouldn't have.

A couple of days later, when Jimmy stood up from his lunch table to go throw out his trash, he had a giant wet stain on the front of his pants that hadn't been there when he sat down. Nobody noticed it at first, until someone from the back of the caf yelled: "Jimmy peed his pants!" The kid who yelled must've had great eyes . . . or a fat wallet.

There were quite a few Jimmys in school, so it took Jimmy Forrester a second to realize that all eyes in the cafeteria were trained on him, or more specifically, the front of his pants. He looked down to confirm his suspicion. When he looked back up, there was an expression of surprise and horror painted on his face in broad, colorful strokes. His eyes darted back and forth, searching for an escape route. But the crowd's laughter bore down on him like a freight train, freezing him in his tracks, forcing a teacher to wade into the crowd to rescue him. Hardly anyone noticed the little girl who had been seated next to Jimmy just a moment earlier: little Nicole Finnegan, with the innocent face, bright red hair . . . and empty juice box. Jimmy had been humiliated, one drop of apple juice at a time.

Jimmy was finished at the Frank. Done. He just didn't know it yet. Or maybe he did know, but wasn't ready to accept it. For the rest of the day, he tried to act like he could still take whatever he wanted from whomever he wanted, but the act was like a five-year-old T-shirt: It no longer fit. It didn't matter how big or tough he was; the entire school had labeled him a loser, a baby, a kid who still wet his pants. He had lost his ability to intimidate, and a bully without intimidation was like a new car without a motor: It may look impressive, but it wasn't going anywhere.

I had to give Jimmy credit: He did try. At one point,

he grabbed a kid who he had terrorized on a regular basis, a kid by the name of Terrell Williams. Terrell was the smallest kid in school, but he also had one of the loudest laughs. When Jimmy threatened to rearrange his face, Terrell let loose his laugh. It rose above the regular middle-school hallway noise. Jimmy was confused by the reaction. Then Terrell sealed Jimmy's fate by whacking him in the place where all boys, no matter what their size, are vulnerable. Jimmy dropped to the floor; any illusion that he was still a bully was suddenly gone.

As Jimmy started to accept the change in his status, his appearance began to change as well. The more ridicule and scorn he absorbed from his classmates, the smaller he tried to make himself. He started to walk with a stoop, his shoulders and arms drawn in. He no longer made eye contact with anyone. Walking, talking, running . . . it didn't matter: His eyes were permanently cast down to the floor. He developed a nervous tic. Nobody, including his old friends, talked to him anymore, unless it was to make fun of him.

Jimmy Forrester had become the founding member of the least popular club in school: the Outs. This club had a highly undesirable method of initiating new members:

humiliation. Vinny was marking the kids that he wanted taken out of the school social system, and the pee stain was the perfect symbol for this. Most kids knew the pee wasn't real, but it didn't matter. Kids laughed at the victims anyway. Why? There's no easy answer to that. Middle school is tough. Everyone's got a reason to be insecure. If someone else is getting laughed at, then that means nobody's laughing at you. And most kids feel like they're always one step away from being the class joke.

Once you were in the Outs, you were there for good. The only kids you could talk to were other Outs. Everyone else treated you with a mixture of scorn and disgust, as if you had a highly contagious disease. I heard about a few kids who convinced their families to move to another town to try to escape the Outs, only to have the tag follow them there. The ridicule was brutal and inescapable. You no longer had any friends, or confidence, or life. Jimmy was the first member; he was by no means the last.

The next victim was Gretchen Jacobson, a popular eighth-grade cheerleader for the school basketball team. Gretchen was like a poorly fed show poodle: pretty, well groomed, and mean. She took great pleasure in embarrassing Vinny, calling him a big, fat pig whenever she saw him. She began to keep track of how big the crowds were at these roasts, like a marathoner keeping a log of her best times. Each Vinny bashing became an attempt to break her witness attendance record.

One morning when Gretchen was wearing her cheerleading uniform—her privilege on days when the basketball team had games—she passed Nicole Finnegan on her way to her locker. Nicole smiled her brightest, sweetest "Hello!" smile, then pulled out two small squirt guns. In a split second, the front of Gretchen's skirt was completely soaked in cat pee. I heard from a reliable source that the squirt guns disappeared so quickly into Nicole's pockets that they might as well have been made out of steam. In fact, Gretchen and my source might have been the only two kids who saw them. Predictably, Gretchen was furious. As she turned to grab Nicole, the call went out:

"Gretchen peed herself!"

Gretchen tried to turn the tide, but it's hard to drown out a hallway full of laughter when you're covered in cat pee. It wasn't long before the tide swallowed her up, leaving her soaked and sobbing. She didn't show up to the game that night, or any other night for that matter. Her "friends" on the squad had turned on her, like lions on a wounded antelope. She had ruined her uniform, which to cheerleaders is worse than burning the flag. They kicked her off the squad. When Gretchen finally showed up at school a few days later, she was a shell of her former self.

News started to spread about Vinny's rise to power, but a lot of kids in school still thought it was a joke. What happened to Dickie Dex, however, proclaimed Vinny's arrival in neon letters too bold to miss: Mess with Vinny Biggs and he will ruin you, completely and absolutely.

It happened on a brisk November afternoon. Nobody thought it was odd that an assembly had been called in the middle of the day, with instructions for the entire school to meet on the playground. The eighth graders were the first to make it outside. Consequently, they had the best view of the fate of their unfortunate classmate. I remember stepping outside and hearing a hundred eighth graders gasp in unison. It sounded like a giant getting punched in the stomach. Then the laughter started. It rolled through the crowd, getting stronger as it moved. I remember craning my neck to see, and finally catching a glimpse of what was left of Vinny's old tormentor.

Dickie Dex was semiconscious, slumped over one of the bike racks on the playground. In his mouth was a pacifier. He was naked except for a diaper, the front of which was soaked with yellow liquid. The back was smeared with a brown substance that suggested that Dickie had no more control of the back functions than he did the front. I heard later through a reliable source that the substance was actually chocolate, but I don't know if anyone that day had the ability or desire to check. From that day forward, Richard Dexter ceased to be the bully known as Dickie Dex; his new nickname was DDD, or Triple D, which stood for "Dirty Diaper Dexter.'" He was so far in the Outs, even the other Outs refused to talk to him.

I remember looking through the crowd that day and seeing a few kids not laughing. Instead they were wearing wide smiles, as if they were watching a repeat of a show they had already seen. Kevin was one of them. So was Nicole. I remember finding Vinny in the crowd, a small grin creasing his chubby face, his eyes cold and set. Then he turned and walked away. The other kids in his crew followed suit. It was a simple act that let everyone know who was responsible. The Franklin Middle School landscape had shifted for good.

Vinny's empire grew. Kids quickly fell into line with the new regime. If they didn't, Vinny had a network of assassins on call, ready and willing to put them in the Outs. Of these hit kids, Nikki was the best, the fastest, the most feared. As her reputation grew, her look and approach began to change. Gone were the pigtails and cutesy dresses. No longer was she the innocent-looking girl who surprised her marks when she took them out. Now she was always dressed in black, her wild red hair flowing behind her. She was fast, sly, and gorgeous—more than a match for her marks. When she walked through the halls, the crowds parted, kids three times her size scrambling to get out of her way. Vinny was the boss, but it was Nikki you feared, knowing it would be her face you saw right before your life took a turn for the worse. She had it all: the money, the notoriety, the power. Then, at the start of seventh grade, she quit.

Nobody saw it coming, except maybe Vinny, who seemed to see everything coming. Three weeks ago, on the first day of school, Nikki showed up looking like every other seventh-grade girl. Her wild hair had been corralled into a ponytail. She was wearing pink jeans and a light green T-shirt. The color made her emerald eyes blaze, the only hint of what might still be lying underneath her new, tamer surface. Kids still treated her like a shark in a school of guppies, but she pressed on with her new agenda. She insisted that everyone call her Nicole and treat her like the past year had never happened. Her request was like trying to win the lottery without buying a ticket: damn near impossible.

Nobody knew how to react. Kevin was especially anxious to talk to her. He had been carrying a torch for her since the moment he met her, giving me at least one reason why Kevin was so eager to join Vinny's crew at the expense of our friendship. Word around school was that Kev and Nikki had been on the verge of going out when summer came. Apparently, he had tried to contact her all summer, but she kept blowing him off. I was at my locker, around the corner from them, when he caught up to her on the first day back, looking for an explanation.

"I'm sorry, Kevin, but I've changed," she said. "I should have told you sooner, but—"

"You're kidding, right?" he shouted. I could have heard him from my house. "What do you mean you've 'changed'?"

"Please don't yell at me."

"I'm sorry . . . I just . . . I don't know what to think. I thought you liked me."

"I do."

"This is not how you act when you like someone."

"I don't think I like you the same way you like me."

"Oh."

"You're a nice guy Kev, but . . ." She trailed off, leaving the sentence open-ended. Only an idiot wouldn't know where that "but" was heading.

"Is it him? Are you seeing him now?" he asked. I held my breath, waiting for a response. Who was "him"?

She didn't answer. "The subject is closed, Kevin," was all she said. There was no mistaking the shift in her voice, from sweet and sympathetic to hard, flinty, and slightly annoyed. Nicole's appearance may have changed, but underneath it all, Nikki was still there. And Nikki wasn't about to be pushed around, no matter how she was dressed.

There was a tense silence, then a sharp *bang* as Kevin punched one of the lockers. I peered around the corner. Kevin's face was bright red. He was breathing heavy and rubbing the knuckles on his right hand. Nicole was staring at him calmly, as if they were discussing an upcoming algebra test. They stayed like that for a full minute, neither of them speaking. Finally, Kevin stormed off, most of his questions left unanswered.

He wasn't the only one Nikki had cut out of her life. She avoided all her past associates, trying to strike up friendships with some of her other classmates. These relationships always seemed forced, as if she was in a play she had never rehearsed and the other cast members were too afraid to tell her that she didn't know her lines.

The reason behind Nikki's sudden transformation was obvious to everyone but the dumbest of kids. She was scared, but not for herself. The day that "Nicole" replaced "Nikki" just happened to be the same day that Nicole's little sister, Jenny, started sixth grade at the Frank. Nicole wanted to shield Jenny from the life she had led, and there was no way to do that if Nikki kept taking jobs from Vinny. It would be like a butcher trying to raise his kid vegetarian.

I didn't have any siblings, younger *or* older, but I knew enough in my time. Older ones tended to want to either guard or lord over their younger sibs, while younger ones just wanted their own lives. This wasn't true in all cases, just most.

As I was mulling all of this over, the bell rang, snapping me back to the present and sending me to my last class of the day. I looked at the clock. Forty minutes until I faced the former Nikki Fingers, the fastest and most beautiful hit kid this school had ever known. Forty minutes for me to reflect on my life and get a few things in order—just in case the job went wrong. I was by no means defenseless, but I was a realist. As good as I was, I was no match for Nikki if she wanted to play rough.

As soon as class let out, I hustled over to my locker and dumped everything inside. My plan was to go to Nicole with empty hands and a clear conscience, and hope that she was in a good mood. I was just about to close my locker door when Elizabeth Carling, Kevin's younger sister, slid up beside me. I only jumped a little bit . . . like four feet.

"Hey, Matt."

"Liz."

She was a year behind Kevin and me, not that it

mattered much. She was smarter and savvier than most kids, and even some of the teachers. Her hair was jet black and cut short in a boyish bob. Her eyes were large and brown; her face was porcelain perfect. She smelled like the first day of spring. Nikki Fingers may have been an exotic beauty, but nobody made my stomach do belly flops like Liz. I had come to realize, months after my friendship with Kevin dissolved, that it was Liz I missed more. She had always hung out with us, eager to join whatever crazy scheme we had thought up, no matter how rough. Kevin would always try to stop her. He doted on Liz, and never wanted to see her get hurt, but she would always ignore him and join us anyway. She was small, cute, and about as fragile as a tanker truck.

"Didn't see much of you this summer," she said.

"I was busy."

"Private-eye stuff?"

"Something like that."

"Humph," she said in the dismissive tone of a queen speaking to one of her subjects. She reached across me and grabbed a pretzel from the bag I kept on the top shelf of my locker.

"Go ahead," I offered, "help yourself."

"I could tell you wanted to give me one. I'm psychic."

"Oh yeah? What am I thinking right now?" We stared at each other as if she were trying to read my thoughts and I was trying to stop her. If she succeeded, I was in trouble.

"You . . . vant . . . to give me . . . another pretzel," she said, trying to sound like a gypsy.

"Wow. That accent is horrible," I said, laughing.

"I curse you and your salty snacks!" She chomped down on the pretzel, chewing violently, with her mouth open.

"Classy. You should do that for your yearbook picture."

She laughed, then chewed a little more discreetly. "So what kind of stuff?" she asked, going back to her normal voice.

"Huh?"

"What kind of private-eye stuff?"

"I can't tell you. Client confidentiality."

"Client confidentiality," she mimicked.

"Sure, make fun of my standards . . . but when you hire me to find your missing model horse, you'll be glad I have them."

"Missing model horse? Ugh. I don't think so."

"Uh, Liz? I've been in your room. You hide them well, but they're there."

"Only so that I'll appear 'girly' enough for my mom."

"Good luck convincing other people of that."

"Point taken." She licked the salt off her fingers. "So why do you do it? The whole private-eye thing . . ."

I shrugged. "Because I'm good at it. The same reason you play chess."

Liz smiled at me. She was a champion chess player, state ranked. Some people said she was a prodigy. Her dad drove her to tournaments twice a month, where she proceeded to beat people three to four times her age.

"I play chess because I love it *and* I'm good at it," she said. "Big difference."

I shrugged.

"Unless you love being a detective . . ."

"I don't discuss love in the school hallway." After I said it I realized that that could have more than one meaning. I quickly turned to my locker. My face felt hot enough to bake cookies on. I grabbed a pretzel, even though the last thing I needed at the moment was something salty . . . all the moisture in my mouth had evaporated. I fiddled with the pretzel for a moment, then gathered my courage and turned back toward Liz.

She didn't seem to notice anything out of the ordinary. She only "humph"-ed again, reached around me, and grabbed another pretzel.

"I think I have some tape in my backpack," I said, trying to regain my composure. "We could tape the bag right to your mouth. Save you the trouble of having to reach for them."

She laughed and threw the pretzel at me. "You're such a gracious host."

"Host? Nobody invited you over," I said with a smile.

"Are you working on a case right now?"

I didn't want to start in with the whole Vinny story. Liz wasn't a huge fan of Vinny's despite, or maybe because of, her brother's involvement. Plus, I wasn't exactly proud of my own compromised principles. "Maybe."

She looked at me suspiciously, as if I were a cat with feathers around my mouth sitting under an empty birdcage. "Client confidentiality?" she asked.

"Possibly."

"Oooh . . . the mysterious Matt Stevens."

"You'd better believe it."

"What if I didn't?" She had a wry smile on her face. She seemed to be inviting me to take a leap, to say something that could move our friendship in another direction. Or maybe she wasn't. Maybe that was just wishful thinking on my part. Between my earlier "love" comment and my impending face-off with Nikki, I was in no shape to judge what was going on between us just then.

"I have to go," I said, saving myself the embarrassment of making the wrong decision. I grabbed the bag of pretzels and tossed them to her. "Something to remember me by." She had a confused look on her face. I closed my locker and walked away before she could ask me another dangerous question.

"See you around, Stevens!" she called out.

I had to push Liz out of my mind and get focused, and there would be no hope of doing that if I turned to look at her again. So I waved without turning around, put my head down, and kept walking.

Nicole's locker was a couple of hallways over from mine. I took my time getting there, trying to get my nerves in check, but it was no use; I was jittery, like a little kid with a three-candy-bar-a-day habit.

I turned the final corner, and there she was: Nicole

Finnegan, standing at her locker with her back toward me, wearing dark brown pants and a beige top. On most girls, brown looked plain and blah. When Nicole wore it, brown became your new favorite color. She was talking to her sister, Jenny. Jenny looked like the kind of girl who longed to be in one of those sappy romance novels—the kind where all she did was ride a horse and make eyes at the handsome stable boy. She was holding a notebook to her chest, the front of which was covered with pictures of horses, and I smiled at the confirmation of my first impression. She was a little shorter than Nicole, with big brown eyes and long hair pulled back into a ponytail. She was definitely cute, but next to her sister, she looked ordinary, like a Ford parked next to a Ferrari.

"You don't know what he's like," Nicole said, softly but firmly.

"Stop trying to control me!" Jenny yelled back. "You already screwed up your own life! Leave mine alone!" Jenny stormed past me, eyes smoldering like fresh bullet holes. Nicole still had her back to me. She hung her head down a little, rubbing her eyes with her hand.

"What do you want, Stevens?" she said, without

looking. It was like trying to sneak up on a three-headed cobra.

"Umm . . . hey . . . uhh, I've got a message from someone." My voice sounded like an equal mix of nerves and puberty.

"Who?" she asked.

"You know who."

She turned to face me. There was something in her eyes that wasn't anger, but was close enough for my taste. "I know you don't mean *him*. He and I have a deal," she snarled. Her left hand moved slowly toward the squirt gun she had concealed in her locker, the one she denied she still had. I raised my hands in the universal sign of surrender, hoping she wouldn't just pop me anyway. I felt like I was on a life raft that was slowly but steadily losing air. If I didn't plug the hole fast, I was going to drown.

"He sent me because he said he respects you, Nikki—"

"Nicole," she said. "I haven't been Nikki for a long time."

I could feel my raft sinking. "Right . . . sorry. Nicole," I stammered. "You have a trinket of his. A good luck charm. He didn't think it meant much to you anymore, so he wants it back."

"And you're here to get it by any means necessary?" Her hand kept moving steadily toward her squirt gun. My life raft was completely deflated now and I was barely treading water. I became distinctly aware of the silence behind me. All action in the hallway had stopped. Kids were trying to decide whether I was crazy or stupid to rile Nikki up. I felt my scalp tingle as I tried to figure out the same thing, but deep down I already knew the answer: I was definitely stupid. I said a silent prayer for my salvation, and followed it up with a silent curse on Vinny and all his descendants. Then I tried to reinflate my life raft.

"It's not like that, Nicole. You know my reputation. He sent me as a white flag. He wants the trinket back, but only if you don't want it anymore. In fact, part of him hoped that you'd want to keep it, as a reminder of what you once had together."

Her hand stayed poised over the squirt gun, twitching a little as if itching to pop someone after months of inactivity. My chest thumped, and I wondered offhand if it was possible for a twelve-year-old to have a heart attack. Suddenly, her hand relaxed and dropped to her side. She smiled a sly little smile that made my heart beat even harder—something that hadn't seemed possible a moment earlier. I managed to recover before my knees buckled, but only just.

"The surfer girl," she said. A light danced in her eyes. She was pleased to remember something that represented the past she obviously missed.

I nodded and smiled back. The crowd behind me let out a sigh of disappointment, then resumed their regular routines. The show was over with no casualties.

"He always used to say it was my good luck charm," she said, "the real reason I made it out untouched."

"I think your quick hands had more to do with it than a good luck charm."

"Maybe, but there's always someone whose hands are quicker."

"True," I said.

She turned to her locker. The move was smooth and graceful, her hair swishing like a rain shower. When she turned back, she was holding a small statuette, no bigger than a pack of gum. It was a hula girl clutching a surfboard. The hula girl was smiling, as if she thought that all she needed was her surfboard and a wave and everything would be right with the world. Nicole was also smiling, but sadly, as if she knew better.

"This is it," she said.

"If you want to keep it, keep it," I said. "I get paid either way."

Her smile remained, but her eyes crinkled in surprise.

"He was pretty adamant about not pressuring you into a decision," I continued. "He only wanted it back if you didn't want it anymore."

Her smile got a little wider as she looked at the little figurine in her hands. She had placed all the memories of her past life into that little smiling surfer girl, and now she was trying to decide if she wanted to part with it. It was the only thing she had left.

"Sometimes I think about the kids I took out, and I really feel bad for them," she said, a note of sweetness in her voice that I had never heard before. Then her eyes hardened. "And sometimes I think of all the kids I *should* have taken out before I quit." I shivered. It was like having a conversation with two different people trapped in the same body.

"Maybe if I give you this, Nikki will go away completely," she said, more to herself than to me. "Then I can just be Nicole." I couldn't tell if the thought thrilled or horrified her. Either way, I knew it wasn't true.

She grabbed my hand and put the surfer girl in it. I felt a jolt when she touched me, like holding a toaster in the bathtub.

"Take it," she said softly. "I don't want to be who I was anymore."

I nodded and closed my hand around the figurine. "Okay," I said. I heard a quick two-pump behind me. Before I could turn around, two giant bursts of water caught Nicole square on the front of her pants, right below her waist.

The blasts were so big, they sounded like watermelons hitting the sidewalk after a ten-story free fall. The surprise and force of the water jolted her backward, causing her head to slam into the locker doors. She slid to the ground butt first, legs splayed, eyes glazed over in shock.

I hit the ground and rolled away, trying to orient myself to the direction of the blasts. The crowd in the hall thickened almost on cue, like a storm cloud blotting out the sun.

"Nikki peed her pants!" someone yelled. Suddenly, I felt the weight of the crowd's eyes, even though they weren't directed at me. I turned back to Nicole. The ominous wet spot stood out clearly on the front of her pants, impossible to miss.

The first peal of laughter came from someone in the back. Like a spark on a pile of old newspapers, the laughter liked what it tasted and started to spread. Soon, the whole crowd was laughing hard. A full year of fear and hatred was fueling it, giving it power. Nicole cringed. She had always known this day would come, and now that it was here, it was worse than she had expected. She let out a soft whimper.

"PEE-PEE PANTS! PEE-PEE PANTS!" the crowd chanted, over and over again, each chant gaining in volume and strength. "PEE-PEE PANTS! PEE-PEE PANTS!"

"Nicole!" came a single cry, only audible because of its difference from the chant. I turned in the direction of the voice and saw Jenny Finnegan fighting her way through the crowd. As she made her way toward her sister, another kid pushed past her in the opposite direction. That kid was the only person moving away from the scene.

"PEE-PEE PANTS! PEE-PEE PANTS!" The roar was deafening.

Jenny sat down next to her sister, tears welling up in her eyes. Nicole was too shocked to move. "Stay with her!" I yelled. I jumped up and started pushing kids out of the way, trying to get to the lone, fleeing figure. It was like trying to dig out of quicksand with a teaspoon. By the time I made it to the outer fringes of the crowd, the kid was gone. I grabbed the boy closest to me. He was chanting with a fervor that bordered on maniacal.

"A kid just passed here!" I yelled in his face. "Who was it?"

"PEE-PEE PANTS! PEE-PEE PANTS!" was his response.

I pushed him aside and ran to the intersecting hallway. The assassin was gone.

I ran back to the scene. The crowd was chanting even louder now, pushing closer. From inside the semicircle, Jenny cried, "Get away from her!" As I was trying to figure out what to do, a hall monitor came around the corner. It was Kelley Diana, a third-year badge who I had met last year while working a case. She was even-tempered, but could get nasty in a hurry. She was going to need to. "Hey! Break it up!" she shouted. The crowd kept chanting, pretending not to hear her.

“Let’s go!” Kelley pushed kids out of her way, sucking energy out of the crowd. “I said, break it u—” Kelley froze in mid-shout when she finally shoved her way to the center of the circle and saw Nikki Fingers lying on the ground, the front of her pants splattered with liquid. Kelley’s mouth hung open. “Holy mother of God,” was all she could muster.

Kids stuck around, hoping that the law could be forgotten just for today. They were about to be disappointed. Kelley turned around, a new ferocity in her eyes, as if she felt guilty for something she had been thinking and needed to make up for it. “Everybody get the hell out of here! NOW!”

Usually when a mob of kids gets broken up, you can see the shame on their faces as they disperse. It’s like they get caught up in the madness of the moment, and once that moment passes, they’re all embarrassed by their loss of control. There was no shame on these kids’ faces, only pure joy. I waded back to Nicole and Jenny. Kelley was still there, calling in backup.

Nicole was completely out of it, as if her mind had hopped on a bike and fled the scene. Jenny, holding her sister’s head in her lap, looked up at me with tear-filled eyes. Her voice was thick with sadness, anger, and disbelief: "Who did this? Who's responsible?"

A bitter laugh slipped out before I could stop it. "She is," I answered, nodding toward the girl who used to be Nikki Fingers.

Within a few minutes, we were surrounded by hall monitors securing the scene, making their reports, doing all the official business they do when it's too late to do anything else. I was asked by five different monitors to give a statement as an official witness, an old trick they used to try to catch kids in a lie. I told them the truth of what happened, leaving out the parts about why I was there, partially to protect my client, partially to protect myself. All the while, Jenny was cradling Nicole in her arms, like the world's biggest newborn. I was replaying the event in my head, trying to recall any clues I might have seen, when Jenny looked up at me. "You're Matt Stevens," she said.

"Yeah."

"I want to hire you."

"Sorry. I don't take revenge cases."

"I don't want revenge."

"What do you want, then? Justice?"

"I don't know," she said in a voice barely above a whisper.

"Let me clue you into something, kid . . . Justice is a snack," I said. "You get justice, and five minutes later you realize you're still hungry. Revenge, on the other hand, is a full meal."

Jenny looked at me blankly. She was too young, too innocent to get what I was saying. Nicole would have gotten it, but she was no longer taking in information from the outside world. Her eyes resembled the eyes of a stuffed animal; they reflected the overhead lights with no indication that they saw them.

"Please," Jenny said, fresh tears flowing down her cheeks. "Please. I'll pay whatever you want. Just find the kid who did this." I left without responding. I couldn't negotiate a price for finding the criminal when I felt somewhat responsible for the crime. Maybe I wasn't in on the plot, but I should have known something was up. Stupidity doesn't make you innocent.

I walked through the halls toward Vinny's locker. Nikki's figurine was in my pocket, the little plastic surfboard scratching my leg with each stride, a constant reminder of what happens to people dumb enough to think there's such a thing as easy money. Kids were buzzing around, spreading the news of Nikki's downfall.

My anger ratcheted up with each step. Most of it was directed at myself, but I felt like I had enough to share with a special someone. Vinny was standing at his locker, getting ready to go home. Brian, a bodyguard roughly the size of Australia, was putting books in a backpack for him. I broke into a sprint. They must have heard me coming because they both turned toward me. Vinny looked nonchalant, as if I were coming to bring him a cup of tea. Brian, whose hands were still full of books, wore an expression of indecisive panic. I hit Vinny at full speed and pinned him against the row of lockers.

"You set me up." I spit the words out, my face half an

inch away from his. I wanted to make sure he knew exactly how I felt.

"That's okay, Brian," Vinny said to his bodyguard. "Don't feel like you have to do anything."

This woke Brian out of his stupor. He plucked me off Vinny like a ripe grape. He only used one hand and I still slid ten feet down the hall. Brian was embarrassed at his previous lack of action, and was about to overcompensate to make up for it. I prepared to get stomped.

Vinny raised his right hand, palm out. Brian stopped in his tracks.

"Now, what was your problem, Matthew?" he asked.

I got to my feet. "You know my problem. You've known it since lunch."

"If you mean Nicole, then you have the wrong idea. I only just found out about it."

"Bull." I reached into my pocket to grab the surfer girl. Brian froze, his eyes as wide as dinner plates. If I had had a squirt gun, I could have taken them both out and been relaxing at home before Brian even moved. Vinny still looked calm.

"Matthew—"

"Why today?" I asked. "Why, after two months, did

you decide you needed this back today?" I tossed him the figurine.

He caught it with both hands. A tear fell slowly down his cheek. "I don't know," he said. "I really didn't think she needed it anymore. I guess I was wrong. I'm sorry, Nikki." Two more tears followed the first.

"Save the act for the Oscars," I said, "because I'm not handing out any awards. You knew this was going down, and you sent me in as a decoy, a distraction so your man could take her out."

"I understand why you feel that way, so I'm not going to hold your accusations against you—"

"How big of you."

"But ask yourself this, Matthew. If I was really so intent on taking Nikki out, would I *really* be that concerned about covering it up?"

I knew he wouldn't be concerned at all. In fact, he'd be broadcasting it, using it to further his own legend. But my mouth was on a roll, saying things before my brain could stop it. "Well, this was probably revenge for something she did while following your orders. So maybe you didn't pull the trigger, but you're as responsible as the kid that did."

"I like you, Matthew, I really do," Vinny replied, as if

speaking to a small, dumb child, "but sometimes you don't have a clue as to what you're talking about. I never forced her to do anything that she didn't want to. All I did was give her an opportunity, an opportunity that she was born for. And she took it. Why? Because she wanted it. She made a choice, and she faced the consequences of that choice."

I didn't say anything, mostly because I felt like an idiot. He was right. It was a losing argument to try to paint Nikki as an innocent pawn.

"Now then," Vinny said, "here's the rest of your money." He handed me a twenty.

"This is ten too many," I said.

Vinny chuckled. "Always honest . . . The extra ten is a retainer. I want to keep you in my employ, to find out who took down Nikki."

"You don't need me for that. With your network, you could have that kid in the Outs in twenty minutes . . . twenty-five tops."

"You overestimate my reach, Matthew."

"I don't think I do. In fact, I may have underestimated it. You could probably find him in fifteen."

"Are you trying to talk yourself out of a job? I *could* find out who did it on my own, but again—"

"Don't give me that garbage about owing me, because I'm still not buying it from the first go around," I said.

"Listen, Matthew, just take the money. Find out who did this and I'll give you another twenty. That's thirty dollars to do a job that I can tell you're itching to do anyway."

"Nicole's sister already hired me."

"This is a free-market society. I'm outbidding her. Tell her she'll get the same results, but she won't have to shell out a dime. Not a bad deal. Or tell her nothing and collect twice on the same job. I don't care. Just find out who pulled the trigger." He turned to leave, then turned back and handed me the surfer girl. "Here," he said, "you need this more than I do."

I pointed to Brian. "Not if *he's* your bodyguard."

"He's not. Anymore."

Brian winced, then shot me a look that could have peeled paint. After a moment, he wandered off, the weight of his failure bowing his shoulders. He gave a final, wounded look back at Vinny as he rounded a corner out of sight.

"You're going to walk through the halls without a bodyguard?" I asked.

"Your concern for my well-being is touching, Matthew. But don't worry . . . I think I'll be all right." He turned and walked off. When he was fifteen feet from me, three kids seemed to materialize out of thin air, forming a protective half-circle around him. One of the kids turned back and blew me a kiss; I doubted she was looking for a date.

I left school with a lot on my mind, but not much in my stomach. It was already four o'clock. I hopped on my bike and rode home, reviewing the events of the day. They rolled around my brain like billiard balls on a table with no pockets; nothing was sinking in.

Nikki Fingers had once been the most feared trigger girl in school, and now she was in the Outs. The number of suspects could fill a New York City phone book. I was having a harder time thinking of kids that didn't have a motive. The question was: Who had the motive *and* the guts? That was a much shorter list. Then again, a kid gets some sugar-induced courage—a couple of sodas, a couple of candy bars—there's no telling what he or she will do.

Take a case I worked on last year. Some kid from the yearbook staff hired me to track down his camera. He had put it in his locker and gone to lunch, and had come back to find it missing. Nothing else was out of place. In fact, his locker door was still locked. The only thing gone was his camera. Turns out, kids from the yearbook staff had had cameras taken from their lockers all year, all with the same M.O.: Kids would go to their lockers after lunch, unlock them as they always did, and nothing would be out of place, except the cameras that were in there before lunch were now gone. The hall monitors didn't have any leads, so they were keeping the story hush-hush.

Instead of attempting to solve the case through the front door, I decided to try a back way. I went to the two camera stores in town that bought used equipment. A lot of criminals in the Frank forgot that when they tried to deal their stuff to the adult world, they always left an impression. Both camera places had bought equipment from a "blond kid, ten to twelve years old, medium height, freckle-faced, tons of energy, and a wide, disarming grin."

They remembered him because they thought it was a little weird that a kid would be able to get his hands on so much camera equipment. I had a feeling I knew who it was, but I had a hard time believing it. The next day at school confirmed it. The description was too spot on.

Peter Kuhn was the least likely kid to do anything criminal. Honor society, basketball star, top of his class. On the surface, Peter was a happy-go-lucky model student, but underneath, he had a dirty little secret: He was a Pixy Stixer. He'd go through two or three packs a day. He'd even drink soda through them, as if they were ordinary straws. It instantly doubled the amount of sugar in your bloodstream. Two Pixy juices a day was enough to send most kids over the edge, bouncing off the walls 'til midnight. By the middle of last year, Peter was hitting the juice six times a day, every day. That kind of habit takes a lot of dough—more than an average kid can get ahold of on a regular basis.

Math was Peter's strongest subject. He had an almost photographic memory, especially when it came to numbers and number series. Turns out, he was seeking out kids who had cameras in their lockers. He would approach them with a cover story, saying he needed help with some question in some subject. Or he might just shoot the crap about the state of the basketball team. As his marks were speeding through their routine of opening their lockers, he was memorizing their combinations, just from a glance. It was pretty impressive. Then, when everyone else was at lunch, he would return to the lockers armed with the combinations, the cameras now easy pickings.

After I brought him down, Peter took a couple weeks off from school to "visit an out-of-town aunt." If his story fooled anyone, I've yet to meet them. He came back a changed kid: quiet, reserved, no Pixy Stix in sight. However, every once in a while you'll see him, eyes crazed, molecules on the verge of flying apart, and you know he's been Stixing. Once sugar gets its claws into you, it doesn't like to let go, and there's no telling what you'll do just to get another fix.

When I got home, my mom was rushing around trying to change from her "secretary clothes" into her "waitress clothes." Ever since my dad disappeared, she's needed two jobs just to keep up. That always gave me a sour taste in my mouth.

"Hey hon, how was your day?" Her question started in the kitchen and ended in her bedroom.

"Fine."

"You're home a little late. Everything okay?"

I winced. My mom was too sweet to say it, but it was obvious that she had been hoping to spend five minutes together before she had to rush out.

"Yeah. Something came up that I had to take care of. A little extra-credit project." It wasn't so much a lie as a half-truth. My mom didn't know about my business. There were too many things about it that I'd have to explain, so for now, it was best to keep her in the dark.

She smiled and kissed me firmly on the cheek. "Straight A's and extra credit. You must get that from your father."

Her smile was still there, but the left side of her mouth dropped a bit. It had been over six years since he vanished, but the wound was still fresh. I changed the subject.

"Did you eat?"

She laughed. "I was just about to ask you that. Who's the parent here?"

"Not a good sign if you're asking me," I shot back.

She giggled and bopped me on the head with the sweater she was holding. "That mouth's going to get you into trouble someday."

"What do you mean 'someday'?"

"Chicken's in the fridge. I'll be home around two. Please don't wait up this time."

"Right."

She shot me a look that told me she knew better. She comes home at two in the morning; I'm awake waiting for her. That's the way it is.

"Love ya," she said, then kissed my forehead.

"Back atcha."

She dropped me a wink then slipped out the door. I went to the fridge, grabbed a chicken leg, and had at it. It disappeared in three quick bites. I was surprised I didn't chew through the bone. My stomach accepted the food and greedily asked for more. I made myself a little plate—more chicken and some rice from a separate bowl (careful to avoid the peas)—and headed down to my office.

As the tenants of the first floor apartment, my mom and I had the only indoor access to the basement. The only other person who went down there was the guy who took care of the building, and judging by the building's condition, he wasn't around very often. It wasn't a big basement, and it was full of boxes that held everything from holiday decorations to toys I don't remember playing with. However, it was big enough for me to carve out a little space of my own. I set up shop by the furnace, which helped to keep things comfortable when the weather turned cold. There was a separate door leading to the outside, which allowed me to see clients without having to traipse them through the kitchen. There was even a phone with its own number. I had no idea who paid the bill, but someone did, because I'd been using it for a couple of years and the phone company hadn't shut it off yet. Once in a while, I'd get a call from some guy looking for "Big A," but every time I'd try to take a message, he'd hang up.

I furnished the place with rich people's junk—stuff that was perfectly fine, but sent to the curb by someone with enough money to get sick of it. I had an old wood desk and matching chair; a beat-up but comfortable sofa with a faded floral slipcover; a couple of lamps; and an old-fashioned radio that had needed quite a bit of elbow grease to get working again. It was my own office: a little dark, a little musty, and totally private—crucial for a business like mine.

I set my plate down on the desk. The room had a warm glow from the sliver of sunset that was sneaking in through the small basement window. I sat down and took a moment to appreciate the perfectly peaceful environment I had in which to enjoy my dinner. I opened my desk drawer and pulled out a scrap of paper, the same scrap of paper I pulled out whenever I was in my office and had a few minutes to myself. On that scrap was written: TMS136P15. It was a clue, or at least I thought it was. The police had found that letter/number series neatly typed on a sheet of paper in the glove compartment of my father's car, which they had found parked in a garage four states away. It was the only thing out of the ordinary they had found.

I ate some chicken and stared at the letters and numbers, running through the list of possibilities that I had already dismissed. License plate number? Nope. Too long. Map coordinates? Nope. Wrong letters. Dewey Decimal? Nope. Way off. Before I could think of any new possibilities, someone started knocking on my door as if they held a grudge against it. I put the scrap of paper back in its drawer, then got up to find out who was so excited to see me.

Before I opened the door, I squinted out the

peephole. I had installed it myself last year, after some tricky business involving a hit kid who made house calls. Tonight, Kevin Carling stood on the other side, glaring at my eye. After the events of the day, I had expected him to come talk to me. I just thought it would keep 'til tomorrow. He obviously didn't. I popped the lock and opened the door.

"Hey, Kev."

He pushed past me into my office. "Matt. What's up?" His face told me that he couldn't care less what was up. He had a definite agenda in mind.

"Nothing," I said. "What can I do for you?"

"What happened today?"

"With what?"

"Cut the crap, Matt," he snapped. He was more on edge than I thought. He looked crazed.

"Nikki's number got punched," I said. "If you're surprised by this, you haven't been paying attention."

"Who did it?"

"I don't know."

"Well, who do you think did it?"

"How the hell should I know?" I asked. "Everybody. Nobody. Both answers seem just as likely right now."

"Cut your smart-aleck crap and give me a straight answer!"

I had had a long day, and I was still hungry. This wasn't my idea of relaxing dinner conversation. "Here's your straight answer. Just about everyone in school had a beef with Nikki, including you. So that narrows the list of suspects down to about three hundred. Surprisingly, in the few hours I've been on this case, I haven't had a chance to question all of them. But hey, no time like the present. Where were *you* this afternoon?"

His face turned the color of a boiled lobster. I thought he was going to rip my head off. Instead, he let out a deep breath and fell back into the floral sofa. I tried to look calm, like I wasn't worried about my health.

"I couldn't protect her," he said.

"The last thing anybody thought Nikki Fingers needed was protection."

"I knew better. She wasn't like that all the time. Trust me."

"I'll have to. Any time I talked to her, she was scary as hell."

"She was scary to me, too, but for a different reason. I liked her, Matt. I mean *liked her* liked her."

"Yeah, I know."

"And up until the summer, I thought she liked me liked me, too. At least that's what she told me."

"You guys make out?"

He sighed heavily. "Yeah. On field day. While the boys were running the hundred-yard dash, we snuck off. Kissed for like five minutes . . ."

"You timed it?"

He ignored me. "I didn't hear from her all summer. I called her every day in June. Then I thought, 'To hell with her,' and stopped calling."

"How long did that last?"

"The rest of the summer."

"I'm impressed," I said.

"Don't be," he said. "It was hard to find time to call her when I was riding my bike in front of her house all day."

"Ouch." We laughed, and I suddenly felt sad. Despite my best efforts, I really missed hanging out with Kevin. I think he felt it, too, because an awkward silence followed. "What happened?" I asked, getting us back on topic.

"I don't know. I can't help but think that it's because of . . . you know . . ."

"Your decision to keep working with Vinny? I know

he looks snappy in a suit, but personally, I would have gone with Nicole."

"I made the choice I had to make," he said. "If you knew what I know, you'd have done the same thing."

"Lucky I'm not as smart as you."

"Don't get all high and mighty with me, Matt. You took Vinny's money this afternoon. That just about cancels out your moral authority."

I had nothing to say to that. It was a thought that had been in the back of my mind all afternoon, and now that it was out in the open, it hurt even more.

"What do you want, Kevin?" I asked. The tension between us was back, full force. "If you want to hire me to find the trigger kid, you're about two people too late."

"Not quite. I don't want to pay you to find him. I want to pay you to give him to me after you do."

"Why? So you can fill his pants with chocolate?"

"Just hand him over to me." His eyes looked as dead as an unfed goldfish's.

"He'd have a better shot if I threw him off a bridge."

"That won't be your problem."

"All this time we've known each other and you still don't have a clue about me. I have a pretty good idea what you'd do to that kid, so if I hand him over to you, I might as well do it myself. And I'm not about to cross that line."

He was off of the sofa and in my face. "And *you* don't know *me* very well. I'll get to him regardless, with or without you. My way, you'll have a little money to show for it."

"Go home, Kev. Vengeance isn't good for your complexion."

"Go to hell, Matt."

He slammed the door on his way out.

I glanced at a photo I kept in a frame on the corner of my desk. My mom had taken it two summers ago. Younger versions of Kevin, Liz, and me smiled and mugged for the camera, each of us holding an oversized ice cream cone. Liz's in particular looked ridiculously huge in her small hand. Kevin and I had teased her that there was no way she was going to finish it before it fell to the ground. She ended up having the last laugh. Both Kevin and I lost ice cream that day, while she polished hers off without a problem. Kevin said later that we had gotten our "just desserts." All of us had groaned while Kevin smiled proudly, knowing that the only reason we were groaning was because we wished we had thought of that horrible pun first.

The moment that photo had captured was typical of our friendship. On the surface, there was nothing special about it: just three kids smiling and holding ice cream cones. Yet I treasured that day, along with all the other days we had spent together, doing "nothing special." I had recently come to realize that it was extremely rare to find friendships in which doing "nothing special" was the most fun thing you could ever hope to do. For a moment, I thought about calling Kevin up, telling him I'd help, and confiding in him that I missed being friends. For a moment, I wanted to go back to the way things were between us.

Instead, I sat back down to eat my dinner. No dice . . . I wasn't hungry anymore. I turned on the radio to see if I could catch the end of the Sox game, but they had already lost to the Twins, 8 to 6. I regarded this as a sign that my day wasn't going to improve, so I went upstairs to bed. I stayed awake until I heard my mom's key in the door, sometime around 2:30. She came into my room.

"Go to sleep," she said, kissing my forehead. She didn't have to tell me twice.

When I woke up the next morning, my mom had already left for work. There was a ten-dollar bill and a note on the counter: "Sorry, hon—I had to get to work early this morning. Quarterly reviews—hooray! Also, I have to go right from the office to the restaurant tonight. Mr. Carling needs me to set up for a party. I won't see you until late. Here's some money. Treat yourself to dinner. Be careful and I love you. Mom."

My jaw clenched and locked. Mr. Carling was Albert Carling, Kevin's father. He was the general manager of

Santini's, the restaurant where my mom worked nights and weekends. His wife, Roberta, owned it, having inherited it from her father, who kicked off before I was born. Kevin always said that if he asked his dad which he loved more, his son or the restaurant, his dad would say his son, but only after giving it a lot of thought.

Mr. Carling was a hard man to get a bead on. When I was friends with Kevin and Liz, I saw him all the time. He was always pretty nice to me, asked me how I was doing in school—all the typical "adult to kid" chitchat. When my mom got a job waitressing at Santini's, he did an abrupt one-eighty, becoming aloof and standoffish. When I was over at his house, he would mumble a half-hearted greeting, then retreat to his office. I thought I had done something wrong. It took me a while to realize it was Mom he didn't like.

Mr. Carling seemed to hold a grudge against her, scheduling her for every holiday, calling her in to work on her days off, giving her the most disgusting and time-consuming cleaning jobs. My mom never gave him the satisfaction of being upset. Whenever he'd get on her, she'd just smile and say, "No problem." She would take all the holidays and extra shifts, saying, "Great! We could use the money." Mr. Carling never saw her come home at two in the morning, dog tired, mentally ticking off the hours before she had to get up to go to her office job, knowing that the sleep she would get wouldn't be enough.

There was definitely something between them, something from their past that I wasn't privy to. Whatever it was, neither of them was talking. I never got a chance to ask Mr. Carling, as my friendship with Kevin was going downhill at the time. I doubt he would have given me a straight answer anyway. I did ask my mom about it a couple of times, but each time she just shrugged her shoulders and changed the subject. I had no leverage on her, no way to make her talk. Plus, she had an annoying ability to see right through all my tricks, the ones that made my peers open up to me even when they didn't want to. I had reached an impasse with her, which as a detective was hard for me to accept. I had no other evidence, no other leads to follow, and I knew that the worst thing you could do on certain cases was to try to force it. So I let it lie. Along with my dad's disappearance, it was the case that was always in the back of my mind.

I picked up the ten-dollar bill Mom had left and brought it into her room. The ugly, ceramic pineapple where my mom kept the rest of her emergency fund was on top of her dresser. I put the ten back inside, then added ten more from the money that Vinny had paid me. It looked like I was taking the case.

I showered, then got dressed, making sure to grab the little surfer girl from out of the pocket of the jeans that I wore the day before. Then I grabbed a quick breakfast and headed out to school.

The place was abuzz with a weird energy, almost like the day before vacation. People walked around with dazed expressions, wide and wild grins pasted on their faces. Everyone wanted firsthand accounts. The number of witnesses tripled as stories flew back and forth. Speculation as to who pulled the trigger was rampant. The odds were five to one on the betting boards that Nikki would show up to school like nothing had ever happened. Whoever set those odds was a criminal; whoever took those odds was an idiot. Nobody showed up to school the day after they were put in the Outs. Nobody. And nobody would know that better than Nikki.

A few people approached me and asked what happened. I put on my best "don't talk to me" face and made my way to my locker. I put the History book that I had neglected the night before on top of the Math book that never even made it home. I grabbed my Spanish book and prepared to make myself invisible for class. The less prepared you were, the less it seemed to work. I closed my locker, turned, and almost ran smack into Liz Carling. She was wearing dark maroon tights and a dress as black as her hair.

"He was a mess last night," she said, as if we were continuing a conversation instead of just starting one.

"Who was?"

She shot me an impatient look. I knew who, and she refused to waste time verbalizing it.

"So? That's not my problem."

Her eyes narrowed into slits. "He's your friend, Matt."

"No, he *was* my friend."

She sighed and rolled her eyes. "Can't you just forget all that and help him?

"Help him do what? Find the kid responsible and rub him out? He's got enough thug buddies to help him do that."

"That's not what he wants . . ."

"Don't be so naive, Liz. What the hell do you think he wants? To give the kid a stern lecture?"

"Look, all I know is that he's really hurting."

"Well, what do you want from me? Tell him to get a hug from his mommy."

As soon as I said it, I was sorry. Liz winced as if stung.

"Nice guy . . . ," she mumbled.

My face flushed. Their mother was a tender subject. If their father's attitude toward people was puzzling, their mother's attitude was a neon billboard: She wasn't fond of anybody, and "anybody" included her immediate family. Her affection was reserved for herself and her money, not Kevin, Liz, or, as far as I knew, Mr. Carling. A hug from Mrs. Carling? Kevin might as well ask the principal if he could borrow his car.

Before I could start my apology, Jenny Finnegan walked over and slapped me across the face. The slap looked dramatic, but there wasn't much behind it. "You jerk!" she yelled, then turned and noticed Liz. "Hi, Lizzie."

"Hey, Jenny. You cut in line."

"Sorry."

"No problem. I'll get him next time. See you around, Matt," Liz said and walked away.

"What the hell was that?" I yelled at Jenny while trying to rub her fingerprints off my face.

"You're working for Vinny?" she yelled back. I looked

down the hallway to see if Liz had heard, but thankfully, she was already out of earshot.

"Not that it's any of your business," I said, "but, yes."

She went to slap me again, but I saw it coming and grabbed her wrist. "Let me go!" she screamed, making us look like a married couple on a daytime talk show. Kids stopped what they were doing and watched. I heard the deep voice of a teacher coming around the corner. I pulled Jenny close to me. There was a yellow ribbon holding her ponytail. She was still clutching her horse-covered notebook. I could smell her soap. It was the same kind Nicole used.

"Pipe down or we're both going to end up in detention."

Mr. Rudolph, an eighth-grade History teacher, turned the corner and walked past us. I pretended that Jenny and I were having a casual conversation. "So you like horses, huh?" I asked and willed her to play along. Either she didn't pick up on my cues, or she didn't want to. She just stared at me with a weird mixture of anger and excitement on her face, as if she had never been this close to a boy before and wasn't sure if she liked it. Lucky for us, Mr. Rudolph must have had something on his mind, because he passed by without giving us a second look. When he was out of sight, I let Jenny go.

"I was going to tell you," I said.

"When?"

"Later today. Give me a break, will ya? I only just got here."

"It's all Vinny's fault."

"What is? The Nikki hit?

She nodded yes, her long ponytail bobbing up and down.

"And what, Nikki's the innocent lamb? Please. You may want to buy that bull because she's your sister, but don't try selling it to me."

Jenny started to say something, but stopped. Her gaze dropped from my face.

"Look," I said, regaining my composure. "As far as I can tell, Vinny didn't have anything to do with it."

"But I hired you first!" There was a little whine to her voice that was starting to get on my nerves.

"Technically, Vinny hired me first. Look, I don't want to take money from both of you for the same job, and quite frankly, I think he has more to give."

“I don’t care what he has. She’s my sister. I want to know who did it.”

“You’ll know, but for free. Not a bad deal.”

“But Vinny will know first, and then he’ll get to the kid, like he gets to everything else in this school. Like he got to you.”

I was sick of being reminded of how I sold out to Vinny. I grabbed Jenny and pulled her close. “Listen, sister. You want the trigger, you work that out with Vinny. I’m sure he wouldn’t mind sharing a piece of him. Me? I don’t care what happens to him. How could I with all you sharks after him? If I had any conscience left, I wouldn’t find him at all, because if I think about it too hard, that’s the only chance this kid’s got.” I let go of her. She looked at me like she wanted to scratch her initials into my face. Then her anger broke, and her regular, innocent expression came back.

“I’m sorry,” she said, “I was up all night with Nicole, and I guess I’m a little edgy.”

“Yeah, you and me both.”

She paused. “I’m not a shark. The only reason I want to know is because Nicole is my sister. I don’t want to . . . you know . . .”

"Put the hit kid in the Outs? He may end up there anyway, no matter what you want or don't want."

Jenny nodded slowly then tried to smile, but her mouth wouldn't let her. She clutched her notebook tighter, as if it gave her comfort. "I don't want him to go . . . there. I'll admit that the other day I did . . . but not now. If someone were to put him there now, I would feel horrible."

"Why?"

"Because I wanted it! I wished for it!"

"So what? Wishes hardly ever come true," I said. Without any warning, my dad's face popped into my head, as if to prove my point. I pushed him out as quickly as I could and tried to focus on the task at hand, but my expression must have given me away.

"Are you okay, Matt?" Despite what Jenny was going through, she was still concerned for me. My opinion of her rose a few notches.

"I'm fine. Listen, when you wished for that, you were upset. Your sister was just put in the Outs. Give yourself a break."

She nodded as if she agreed with me, but I could tell by her expression that if the hit kid ended up in the Outs, she would always feel a little responsible.

I noticed for the first time that she was wearing a light blue cardigan; it made her eyes look bluer than a cloudless October sky. My initial evaluation of her looks wasn't quite accurate. She was more than just cute; she was beautiful, with a much softer touch than her sister.

"Just so you know," I said, "Vinny hired me to get this." I took the surfer girl out of my pocket. "But only if your sister was willing to give it up."

She gasped a little. "May I . . . hold it?" I put the figurine in her outstretched hand. "Nicole never let me touch it," she said, her voice tinged with a mixture of awe and bitterness. "She used to say that it only had so much good luck and she needed every drop. Kind of funny that she got hit as soon as she handed it to you."

"Yeah. What were you two arguing about, right before she got hit?"

"Vinny had come up to me at my locker that morning, to welcome me to school," Jenny said, still focusing on the surfer girl. "He was different than I expected."

"You'd never met him before?"

"No. My sister wouldn't let me. If you didn't already

know, Nicole is a bit of a control freak." Jenny handed the surfer girl back to me. "When she realized she couldn't stop Vinny from talking to me, she exploded."

"You looked like the one doing the exploding."

Her eyes were watchful. "Nicole exploded all right, just quietly."

"You stormed off. Why'd you come back?"

"Honestly? To yell at her some more. I don't like people telling me what to do. When I saw her on the ground, at first I . . ." She paused to get the words right. "I felt guilty, because I felt vindicated, like I had won the argument. She got hit because she wasn't a good person. She had no right telling me what to do."

"Harsh."

"I know. I wish I could say I felt something different, but I can't. We can't always help what we feel." She looked up at me. There was an unexpected spark between us. I started to wonder if Jenny was as innocent as she looked.

"So you weren't hired to distract Nicole?" she asked.

"No. I distracted her, but not on purpose."

"I'm sorry . . . I don't mean to keep bringing it up, it's just . . . well, I didn't know what to think. All sorts of scenarios ran through my mind." As she spoke, her ponytail swung back and forth. "I started to think you were in on the hit, and that now you were just stringing me along, ripping me off."

"I'd have slapped me, too."

"Just talking to you now, I know it's not true." She gave me a smile full of sweetness and warmth. "I'm glad it's not true."

There was another spark. I spoke before it ignited something. "And now you get my services for free."

"I want to pay you."

"You don't have to. It's being taken care of."

"I know, but I want to. Vinny takes care of everything in this school. *I* want to take care of my sister. You can still take his money. I can't pay you much, but I want to pay you something. I want to know that I at least contributed to finding out who did this."

"I understand."

"So, how much?"

"Let me find the perp first. Then you can pay me according to how hard you think I worked."

Her smiled widened. "You're an unusual boy, Matt Stevens." She kissed my cheek—the same one she had slapped earlier.

"Uhh . . . thanks . . . ," I mumbled. All of a sudden, my palms were sweaty and my tongue felt three sizes too big for my mouth. I peeled my gaze away from the floor and forced myself to look at her. She blushed deeper than I had ever seen anyone blush before.

"Jenny," someone said, interrupting us. The voice belonged to a girl who looked familiar to me, but I couldn't place her. She was a hall monitor; that much was clear from the sash she was wearing. It looked to be the right size, but still didn't seem to fit well. "We have to get to class," this girl said, in a way that made it clear that she didn't approve of the moment Jenny and I had just shared.

"Just a sec, Mel," Jenny responded. "I'll see you later, Matt?"

"Sure."

Jenny smiled, then turned to join her friend. Her ponytail bobbed jauntily as she and "Mel" walked off together. I could still feel her kiss . . . and her slap. I wasn't sure which left a deeper impression.

By lunchtime, I still hadn't found any useful information. I decided to question some of the kids who were in the crowd when Nikki got hit. The first two I went to were Jeremy Farmer and Todd Lundgren. Last year, their friend Bobby Higgins had placed a bet on the basketball team to win, with money he didn't have. Our team lost the game—badly—and Bobby had been too broke to pay up. He tried to bargain for more time, claiming that his birthday was coming up. It was . . . in eight months. Vinny sent Nikki to give him an early present. Jeremy and Todd tried to hang around with him afterward, but it was no use. Bobby was in the Outs now, and no longer the kid they had been friends with. Apparently, they still missed him, because when I asked Jeremy and Todd about Nikki, they clammed up tighter than a cheap lady's purse.

Next I went to Nancy Pilkenton. Nikki took Nancy's sister out last year. Nancy wasn't talking, either.

"I didn't get a good look at him," she said, her mouth full of tuna sandwich.

"He walked right past you."

"I didn't notice. I was a little busy at the time."

"Busy yelling at Nikki."

"That's right. What of it? She took my sister out for no reason, you know. Nikki deserved what she got."

The smell of tuna was turning my stomach. "Your 'innocent' sister was bullying sixth-grade girls for their lunch money."

"What the hell do you know? Scram. Unless you want to give the kid a medal, I didn't see nothin'."

I approached a bunch of other kids that I recognized from the scene of the crime, but like an English teacher in a room full of cheaters, I kept getting the same story.

Nobody saw anything. All of them had friends or relatives that Nikki had taken out; none of them wanted to help bring down the kid who got her. I was about to give up when the bell rang, taking the decision out of my hands. I packed up my half-eaten lunch, grabbed my books, and headed for Algebra.

As I was walking, a kid caught up to me and kept pace. His name was Steven Beckett. I knew him from class. He looked like he had something on his mind.

"Hey, Matt."

"Steve."

"You got a minute?"

"Maybe. Class is starting in five."

"I know. I sit two rows behind you."

"Right. Can you talk while we walk?"

"Yeah," he said, then stopped walking. His mind and his mouth seemed to be on different tracks. I stopped, too. It seemed important.

"What's going on, Steve?"

"I saw who did Nikki."

Before I could say anything, he spoke again.

"Well, I didn't see him. I heard him. As he passed by."

"What did you hear?"

He paused. “Nikki took out my brother, you know,” he said. His shoulders sagged.

“Yeah, I know.”

Steven’s brother Jeff was scum. There was no way to sugarcoat it. He was one of those bullies who had a hard time believing Vinny could put him out of business. Vinny let him know that he could. Jeff pushed; Vinny and Nikki pushed back harder.

“He had it coming,” Steve said. “He was no good.”

“I know that, too.”

“He used to beat on me. A lot. He even had a nickname for me: Sissy Boy. He called me that all the time, even at school.” A single tear rolled down his cheek. “Do you know what it’s like, to be humiliated every day and not be able to do anything about it?” he asked. I didn’t answer. I had no idea.

“At first, after Nikki took him out, I wanted to thank her, give her a hug, not that I could get close to her. She had done to Jeff what I had always dreamed of doing.”

I nodded. This had been on his mind for a long time.

“Jeff was like a different person afterward: quiet, watchful, nervous. He wouldn’t speak unless spoken to. He jumped at every little sound. It was like living with a frightened animal. As much as I didn't like him before, I liked him even less after. And things didn't change when he got to high school. If anything, they got worse."

"If you're withholding info in service to your brother," I said, "just realize he would never do the same for you. He doesn't deserve your pity."

"You think I don't know that?" he cried out. "But you don't see him every day, the way he looks . . . the way he acts." He shuddered. "I don't know if I can tell you what I know and look at my brother every day . . . knowing that I helped get justice for Nikki after what she did to him."

The bell rang. He tried to look at me, but closed his eyes instead. He knew he'd be ashamed of either decision he made.

"I heard a voice," he said. "Small, high-pitched, and weasely."

"Female?"

"No, male. Definitely. I could've imitated it for you last year, but my voice changed."

"What did he say?"

"'Yeah . . . That got her . . . yeah . . .'"

"Is that all you heard?"

"No. There was something after it."

"What?"

He tried to hold back, but the answer leaked out of him. "It was a giggle . . . a high-pitched giggle."

I didn't say a word, just carefully exhaled. Steven looked at me, disappointed. "You know who it is."

"Not really," I tried to lie. "No."

"I was kind of hoping it wouldn't be useful."

"It wasn't."

"I'll tell that to the face in the mirror every morning," he said, "but I don't think he'll believe it, either."

I spent the rest of the day looking for Joey "the Hyena" Renoni, but he was harder to find than a hot dog in a health food store. As far as I knew, nobody else had the information I had, but I knew it wouldn't be long before word got around. News traveled fast, especially to kids like Vinny and Kevin. Finding Joey was priority one; checking in with my clients was the furthest thing from my mind. Unfortunately, Jenny had other plans. At the end of sixth period, she was standing at my locker, that same horsey notebook in her hands.

"Hi, Matt."

I looked past her. Her friend Mel was a couple of steps away, her hall monitor's sash glowing an unnatural orange. She was watching us with the same disapproving look that she wore the first time I saw her. "Jenny," I said, "you should get to class."

"Have you found anything out yet?"

"Nothing I'm prepared to talk about right now."

"Why not?"

"I'm just not, Jenny. Look, you're paying me to do my job, my way."

"I know," she said, a big pout on her face. "I just . . . I can't concentrate in class. I can't . . ." She sniffled and covered her eyes, then took a deep breath and slowly exhaled. She clutched her notebook again. She was trying to keep it together. "I can't think about anything else."

"I know, and I'm sorry. But I'll tell you things when I'm ready to tell them. If you don't like it, you can hire someone else."

"No. Please, I'm sorry. Don't be like that, Matt." She touched my arm, more as a reflex than anything else, but once her hand was there, it felt right. She let it linger for a moment, then slowly pulled it away.

"Listen," I said, "take it easy. All I have right now are shadows. As soon as I have something of substance, you'll be the first to know."

"Okay. I'll see you later?" she said while walking backward away from me.

"Maybe. I've seen you twice today, and neither time went very well."

"Maybe the third time's the charm," she said, then turned deftly on her heel and glided down the hall toward her waiting friend. Her ponytail flipped playfully behind her. It was an impressive and fluid motion, one that made you want to hang around with her just so you'd have a chance to see it again. I allowed myself a moment to commit it to memory, then continued my search for Joey.

I finally caught up to him about a half hour later. He was outside behind the building, pitching pennies out of sight of the recess-sanctioned game of kickball. He was taking money from a couple of suckers when I came up behind him.

"I need to talk to you," I said.

"Oh yeah? Hehehe." His hand moved toward the squirt gun in his pocket. I bull-rushed him, pinned his arms to his chest, and pressed him against the wall.

"Leggo a me! Hehe!"

"I'm doing you a favor," I replied through gritted teeth, "and I'm not going to get popped because of it."

"Whatta you want, a kiss—oww!" I moved his arms at an uncomfortable angle.

"Shut up and listen. I'm taking you to the principal."

"On what charge? Taking these kids' money? They wanted to play. Just ask them. Hehehe."

I didn't ask them. Instead, I told them to beat it.

"How'd it feel, taking Nikki out?" I asked Joey when the kids were gone.

"What? Hehehe."

"You heard me."

"The only thing I took out was your mom. Hehehe—owww!" I twisted his arms.

"I've got a witness. Says your giggle was fleeing the scene."

"You were fed a bum line, jerk. I wasn't there. Hehehe."

"Tell it to the principal."

"Leggo a me! I didn't do nothin'! Hehehee!" He squirmed but I held him fast.

"Innocent's not a good fit for you, Joey."

"If I popped Nikki, why would I lie to you, huh? You ain't no monitor. Hehehe . . ."

"I don't know. Maybe you just like lying."

"Yeah, lying with your mom. Hehehe," he said, then spit in my face.

"All right." I let go of him. He went for his water gun. "Good luck with Kevin," I said.

His hand stopped. "Kevin?"

"Yeah. He must've talked to some witnesses by now, and it's not like anyone else giggles like you," I said, wiping my face. "So I imagine he'll probably want to discuss your role in the Nikki take-down. And by discuss, I mean beat you to a bloody pulp."

"I didn't do it!" he yelled. "You tell Kevin I didn't do it! Hehehe!"

"You tell him. I have to go wash my face."

"No! Hee! Look, hehe! Here!" He reached into his pocket. I grabbed his arm and twisted it behind his back. "Owww! Owww! Quit it!"

It wasn't a squirt gun in his hand; it was an envelope. I took it and let go of his arm.

"I found it in my locker two days ago. Hehehe."

I opened the envelope and pulled out three pieces of paper: half of a picture ripped out of an old school newspaper, a well-forged hall pass, and a note. In the picture, a younger Joey stared up at me with a goofy, love-struck grin on his face. He was holding hands with a girl, I assumed, but I couldn't tell who. Her hand was in the picture, but the rest of her was in the missing half. The note said: "Remember what we had. Do it or get out of the way. —B."

"What is this?" I asked.

"A note, from a girl I use ta see. Long time ago . . . back in fifth . . . She sent me a different note last week, wanted me to pop Nikki. Hehehe."

This was a new wrinkle. "Is this just to cover yourself, in case you got caught?"

"I ain't that crafty. It's the truth! I said I'd think about it. I was still thinkin' when Nikki got popped!"

"Who sent it?"

He stopped dead.

"Who, Joey? Who was she?" But Joey wasn't paying attention to me anymore. He was focused on the two burly kids coming up behind me. I turned to face them, just in time to be thrown aside like an old newspaper. They grabbed Joey and lifted him off the ground.

"Kevin needs to talk to you about something."

"No . . . hehehe . . . guys . . . *noo!* Hehehe! I didn't do nothin'! Guys! Hehehehe!"

They dragged him off. He screamed and giggled the

whole time. Not one of his screams was the name of the girl who sent him the note.

I picked myself up off the ground and ran after them, but it was too late. By the time I turned the corner, they had dragged him into the equipment shed on the other side of the playground, out of sight of the teachers and other students. A couple of moments later, Kevin came out of the shed. He looked pleased with himself, as if he had just removed a painful splinter.

"Hey, Matt. How's it hangin'?"

"Stop, Kev! You're taking out the wrong kid! Joey didn't do it!"

"Didn't do what?"

"Joey didn't take Nikki out!"

"Oh, he took her out, all right. Joey's always had a thing for Nikki. Talked about her all the time. He thought he was fast enough to take her, and you know what? He was right. He was fast enough. He just wasn't prepared for the consequences."

"No, Kev, you got the wrong story. Joey was set up!"

"Forget it, Matt. I talked to five different kids. They all heard the same thing: Joey whispering 'That got her,' then that freaky giggle of his."

"Yeah, I heard the same story."

"Great. So we agree."

"No, we agree on what those kids heard, not who said it."

"Listen, Matt, I know you like to make things difficult, just so you can feel needed, but this is open-and-shut. Just admit it . . . you're upset because I solved your case."

"No, idiot. You didn't solve a damn thing! Now call them off!"

"Little too late for that." Kevin said. I looked over his shoulder and saw the end of Joey "the Hyena" Renoni.

The expression on his face was of pure horror, not that anyone was looking at his face. All he was wearing was a pair of white socks and an oversized diaper, the back stained a hideous brown. Instantly, the kids in the playground formed a tight circle around him, laughing and pointing, their once-heated kickball game now forgotten.

"Crappy Pants! Crappy Pants! CRAPPY PANTS! CRAPPY PANTS!"

Joey tried a few times to flee the scene, but a couple of big kids kept him where he was. Kevin wanted his money's worth.

"CRAPPY PANTS! CRAPPY PANTS! CRAPPY PANTS! CRAPPY PANTS!"

"Stop!" Joey screamed. As a response, someone hit

him in the face with the kickball . . . hard. Joey started crying. Someone pegged him with the kickball again, this time on the back of his head. He hit the ground on all fours, his brown, stained butt sticking up in the air. This made the crowd laugh louder, and Joey cry harder. "Please," he pleaded. The ball struck him in the face again. His head snapped back, then hung down, tears dripping off it onto the ground. He was sobbing now, but the crowd wasn't about to show him any mercy. Instead, someone found another kickball. Now they were pelting him two at a time. Joey curled up, sobbing and whimpering, the hollow sound of the rubber balls echoing through the playground as they ricocheted off his bare back, his sides, the back of his head.

Five minutes doesn't seem like a long time, unless you're on the playground getting hammered with kickballs, wearing only socks and a stained diaper. Then five minutes is an eternity. That's how long it took for a teacher to finally break things up and get Joey inside. Five minutes to destroy a kid's life. Even the teacher who saved Joey had a look of disgust on her face.

I turned back to Kevin. He looked completely amused, as if he had just seen a comedy act instead of the complete obliteration of a kid's life. "You were saying?" he asked.

"You know, Kev, I used to think there was hope for you, that one day you'd wake up and realize that being Vinny's chump isn't worth it. But I was wrong. You actually like it. You're as big a jackass as he is."

"Whatever you say, champ. In the spirit of our past friendship, I'm going to let your little speech slide. The next time you talk to me like that, you'll get to see the Outs from the inside."

"Oh yeah? Well, in the spirit of our past friendship, here . . ." I put up my middle finger.

He laughed. "See you around, Matt," he said and sauntered off.

I stood there, frozen with anger. Kids walked past me, still laughing about Joey. He had been a rat, and a jerk, and he had put a bunch of kids in the Outs, but I still felt horrible for him. Nobody deserved what he had just gone through. Nobody. I had the sudden urge to grab each laughing kid and wet the front of their pants, just to see how they liked it—to see if they'd still think it was funny. I took a deep breath and tried to pull myself together. When my anger subsided a little, I started walking to the nurse's office. I still needed to talk to Joey.

"Not going to happen," the nurse said to me, her voice hoarse from too many cigarettes.

"Just for a minute," I pleaded.

"Beat it. Get to class." She slammed the door in my face. I walked around the corner and waited. Twenty minutes later, a tall scarecrow of a woman walked briskly into the nurse's office. She looked exactly like Joey, if he were older and dressed as a woman, so I went out on a limb and guessed it was Joey's mom. She slammed the office door behind her, hard enough to rattle the two baby teeth I had left. She proceeded to yell for about ten minutes. The door muffled most of the specifics, but the gist was easy to make out: She was a little upset. Suddenly, the door opened and Mrs. Renoni stormed out, dragging Joey behind her like a tin can on a wedding car.

They were almost out of the building when I caught Joey's attention. He looked at me with the most pitiful expression I'd ever seen. I almost asked him who the girl was that sent him that note, but the question froze on the tip of my tongue. Then he was gone.

For the rest of the day, I kept looking over my shoulder, half expecting the burly kids who dragged Joey off to be standing there, telling me that I had insulted Kevin for the last time . . . telling me that my time was up. In my mind, I would fight them off valiantly, beating them single-handedly as every attractive girl in school watched, cheering me on. Of course, when the last bell rang, I sprinted out of the building like a greyhound out of the starting gate. If they were coming, they'd have to outrun me.

When I got home, my mom was still at her day job, so I went down to my office to have a closer look at the photo, the pass, and the note that Joey had given me. I turned on my task light and grabbed a magnifying glass, feeling a little like a bad cliché in a Sherlock Holmes story. The first thing I looked at was the torn photo, searching for any small detail I might have missed with the naked eye. Nothing. Even though it wasn't my style, I knew I was going to need some help. I picked up the phone and called Jimmy MacGregor, editor of the school paper. He picked up on the first ring.

"This is Mac."

"Jimmy, it's Matt."

"Hey, Matt. What's shakin'?"

"My hands from too much candy. Listen, you think you can do me a favor?"

"Today? Ha! Maybe you heard? Two biggest news stories of the century hit on back-to-back days."

"Yeah, I heard. In fact, I had front-row seats."

"Oh yeah?" he said, so eagerly I thought he was going to come through the phone. "You want to make a statement?"

"Maybe. You want to do me a favor?"

"Maybe. If it's taking an ugly cousin out for ice cream, my social calendar's pretty full."

"I don't have any cousins. I have half a school newspaper picture. I need the other half."

"My paper?"

"Is there any other?"

"Hmm. What's the picture of?"

"I'll show it to you." I looked at the clock on my desk. 5:50. "Be at Sal's in half an hour."

"I can't right now. Bring it by tomorrow, with your statement."

"It's gotta be tonight."

He paused for a second. I heard him shuffle a few papers around. "Does it have to do with Nikki and Joey?" he tried again.

"Off the record?"

"Yeah."

"I'll see you at Sal's."

"Fine, yeah, okay. See you at Sal's." He hung up.

I put the phone down and picked up the day's edition of the school paper. Jimmy Mac must have photocopied liked a fiend, because even though it was only a few hours ago, there was Joey the Hyena on the front page. The picture was blurred, obviously taken in a hurry, but you got a full view of the main event. Joey's eyes were the size of dinner plates. Even in black and white you could see the stains on his diaper. I crumpled up the newspaper and threw it in the wastebasket. I had enough visual images of Joey's destruction to last me several lifetimes.

I picked up the hall pass from Joey's envelope, opened the top left drawer on my desk, and pulled out the hall pass that Vinny had given me yesterday. Both signatures were supposed to be Mr. Allan's, the school's lone Science teacher. All it took was a glance to tell that the same person had forged both of them. Whoever did them was smart to use Mr. Allan, since his signature would work across all grade levels. I picked up the phone and called Vinny.

"Hey, it's Matt."

"Hi, Matthew. Shame about Joey."

"Yeah," I said. "It's a bigger shame than you think. He didn't do it."

"Didn't do what?"

"Play shortstop for the St. Louis Cardinals. What do you think?"

"Nikki? Are you sure?"

"Close to it. Listen, that hall pass you gave me yesterday, where'd you get it?"

"What hall pass?"

"The one you gave me so that I could 'eat my lunch in peace.' "

"I have no idea what you're talking about."

"You know, the fake hall pass."

"Do you always accuse your clients of illegal activity?" he asked, his voice full of understated menace.

I almost answered, "No, just the guilty ones," but stopped short. It rarely happens, but sometimes my survival instinct is able to leapfrog my smart-ass instinct. Vinny wasn't fond of being linked to illegal activity, even in a phone call, at night, nowhere near school property. I beat a hasty retreat. "My mistake. Can I meet with you at some point tomorrow? I have some things about the case I'd like to discuss."

"Oh, we'll meet, Matthew. But I'm not sure you'll like everything I have to say." He hung up.

I felt a tingle on the back of my neck, which was my body's way of telling me that I just screwed up. It's never a good sign when your client threatens you, especially when that client is Vinny Biggs.

I tried to put all that out of my head for now. I pulled the surfer girl figurine out of my pocket. It had been scratching my leg all day.

"You're a good luck charm? So far, I'm not impressed."

Her mute smile seemed to say, "Well, *you* haven't been hit yet."

I put her back in my pocket. She had a good point.

I picked up the two fake hall passes and stared at them, looking for any pattern that would help identify the writer. I reached into my filing cabinet and pulled out my report card from last year. On it was Mr. Allan's real signature. I compared it to the two fakes. The only thing that gave the fakes away was the loops in the letter "L." They were a little bigger than the authentic ones. Fantastic. The key to the case was bigger "L" loops. All I needed were handwriting samples from the entire school and I'd have this case solved by the time I graduated high school. I sighed and checked the clock: 6:10. I went out the cellar door, grabbed my bike, and rode toward Sal's.

Sal Becker was a classmate of mine who ran a little place where kids could grab a sandwich and a soda, without all the hassles kids face in grown-up establishments. It was just an old tool shed, but Sal and his dad spent one summer putting in a bar and some tables. They made it look nice, not too showy, just a simple place where kids could unwind after a long day. The menu was pretty limited: either a peanut butter and jelly sandwich (strawberry or grape) or a toasted cheese, washed down with either a root beer or a cream soda (the good kind in the glass bottles). Two sandwiches and a drink would run you just three bucks. Not bad on a kid's salary.

The cool air felt good on my face as I pedaled. It wouldn't be long before you'd see piles of leaves in people's yards, pumpkins on their steps, and cardboard monsters on their doors. You could already catch a hint of wood smoke in the air, like a whispered promise of things to come. That smell always reminded me of the clearest memory I had of my father. I was seven at the time. We were outside at twilight, laughing as I tried unsuccessfully to catch a football. My dad would throw it, I'd open my arms, and the ball would sail past, my arms not even close. Or the ball would bonk me on the nose. It was one of the foam ones, so it never hurt.

"Hell of a catch, there," he'd say, then we'd laugh hysterically. Someone walking past might think that he was being cruel, making fun of his young son. They would be missing the mark. It wasn't my ability to catch a ball that we were bonding over, it was my ability to catch his sarcasm. He refused to talk down to me. He was telling me that the intellectual playing field between us was even. When I threw the "Hell of a catch, there" back at him as he dropped a couple of passes, he'd wince and laugh, and shoot me a look that told me I had gotten him. I loved him for that.

We tried to get as many throws in before Mom called us for dinner. It was a perfect evening, and as you get older, you start to realize just how few of those you have in your life. Don't get me wrong—life is full of really great moments. But the number of perfect ones, where all the colors and sounds and smells combine in a way you can't quite believe is real, but wish would last forever: Those moments are much more rare.

By December, my dad had vanished. Over the years, my memories of him have gotten fuzzier and fuzzier; all except for the one of us playing ball and goofing on each other. I relive that memory every fall, when the air gets a little chilly and someone in town lights up their fireplace for the first time.

When I got to Sal's, I dropped my bike and waited a couple of minutes before going in. The brisk air had made my eyes tear up. I wiped them on the sleeve of my sweatshirt, took a deep breath, and walked inside.

Sal's place was just the right temperature to take the chill out of you, all thanks to the two portable heaters he had going. The place smelled like toasted cheese and tree sap, a combination that I wouldn't necessarily think to put together, but it worked just fine. I climbed onto one of the bar stools.

"Hey, Matt."

"Sal."

"What'll it be?"

"Two cheeses and a cream soda."

"Comin' up."

He put my sandwiches in the small toaster oven he kept behind the bar, popped the top on my soda, and put it in front of me. I took a swig, then turned and looked around the room. The walls were natural wood paneling, covered with posters of local sports heroes. The floorboards were a few shades darker than the walls, due to age and heavy traffic patterns. A couple of floor lamps gave the room a warm glow that was easy to settle into.

Being that it was a school night, the place was pretty quiet. My only company was a pair of eighth graders sitting at a table in the corner. They looked like they were lamenting a test they had taken earlier in the day. Sal came by and put down my sandwiches. I thanked him, then checked my watch: It went from 6:19 to 6:20. As it did, the door to Sal's opened and in walked Jimmy MacGregor. He was tall for a fourth grader; unfortunately, he was in seventh. His hair was black and sat in tight curls on his head. His skin was light brown and looked like it had been hit with a freckle stick. He walked briskly and sat on the stool next to mine.

"Hey-Sal-what's-shakin'-I-needa-root-beer-and-an-sbpbj-no-crust-lightly-toasted-thanks-man! Hey-Matt-what's-the-story-kid-you-gotta-photo-for-me-to-peep-or-what?" When Jimmy was anxious, he talked fast, like a hyperactive kid on a soda bender. I passed the torn news photo over to him. He studied it for a second.

"That's from an Ellie paper."

"When?"

"Fifth, I'd guess." Sal came over and put Mac's sandwich down in front of him. "Thanks, Sal." Sal nodded and walked away. Mac took a bite, then looked at the photo again. "I remember this. Spring of fifth, right before we moved on to the Frank. They had some kind of end-of-school dance to celebrate us leaving."

"The Spring Fling."

He snapped his fingers. "The Spring Fling! Right! I was there doing a little 'Smile here!' and 'Look casual,' trying to get some stuff for the paper. Total fluff, man, and on the front page. Well, to be fair, there wasn't much to report on in Ellie. First through fifth is a total snooze-fest, news-wise."

"Who was in the missing half?"

"Don't know. I remember the circumstances, not the details. I don't even think I took that picture. Plus, Joey was a total hound back then. A different girl every day."

"Him?"

"Yeah. Chicks dig the bad boy. Plus, the dating scene in Ellie is totally different than here, right? 'Going out' meant you might hold hands on the playground. *Pff.* Big deal. It didn't mean anything then . . . not like it does now."

"Right. You think you can find the other half of this?"

"Sure . . . sure. I'll have to do a little digging, but I think so."

"How long?"

"Couple of days, tops."

I grimaced. Two days might be too long.

He read my expression. "Could be quicker than that," he said. "But it may not. I've got to search through some boxes in the garage. Why, what's the matter?"

"I don't figure Joey for the Nikki hit."

I got a good view of Jimmy's half-chewed PB and J. "Joey didn't do Nikki?"

"No, and keep it down, would ya?" I said.

"Why? As far as everyone's concerned, the story's as cold as frozen tater tots. Cut-and-dry case of school-yard justice."

"Right. And everyone thinking that is just fine with me. Allows me to work under the radar for a while."

"Gotcha . . . gotcha . . ."

"But I've got to move on this quick. It's already Tuesday. I've got three more days to solve this thing."

"What do you mean?" he asked.

"Come on, Mac. You know as well as I do that in the Frank, the weekend's like a reset button. If this thing drags out 'til Monday, I might as well just let the assassin go."

He nodded. "Yeah. Good point. So where'd you get your info?"

"Joey told me, right before his number came up."

"Hardly a reliable source," he said, and took another bite of his sandwich. "Whatcha think, he was just gonna confess?"

"Well, yeah. I went at him because I had an eyewitness who fingered him at the scene. My theory was pretty simple . . ."

"He took out Nikki to take her place."

"Right. Except when I put it to him, he denied it. Then he gave me that photo, along with these."

I slid over the note and the hall pass.

"'Do it or get out of the way,'" Mac read. "Any chance he . . ."

"Wrote that note himself, concocted the whole story, just to take himself off the hook?"

"Yeah."

I shook my head. "He's not that smart. Plus, it doesn't make sense. You know Joey, right?"

"Yeah. He freaks me out."

"Yeah, he freaks everybody out. He's really cocky . . . *was* really cocky. If he did Nikki, there's no way he'd deny it. In fact, you'd have a hard time shutting him up about it."

"Well, maybe afterward he lost his nerve."

"You're telling me he worked up the nerve to take Nikki Fingers out, but lost it when it came time to take credit?"

"Yeah. I see your point." He looked at the note again. "Who's 'B'?"

"Some girl Joey used to see. If Joey was as big a hound as you say he was, it's going to be hard to track her down. The other half of that photo is the best lead I've got."

"I'm on it." He took his last sip of soda, then slid off the stool.

"And listen," I said, "you can't run this yet."

He looked at me as if I were slow in the head. "This isn't amateur hour," he said. "If I run this story now and it turns out to be bunk, I look like a jerk."

"That hasn't stopped people before."

"Yeah, I know . . . Grab the readers *now!* Who cares if you make a mistake and ruin some kid's life? Apologize for it later! And those apologies usually end up on page eighteen, in type so small you'd need a telescope to read 'em. Other kids may feel okay doing that, but not me."

"Yeah," I said. "I know."

"Then why say anything?" he asked, but he wasn't

really mad. He was smiling. I returned it. Mac was honest, and at the Frank, that was as rare as a decent lunch from the cafeteria. "Just promise me the story when it's done."

"Who else would I go to?"

"Good point," he said. "Listen, I still have an hour before my dad gets home. I could root around the garage for a while without having to play Twenty Questions." He threw three bucks on the counter. "See ya, Sal," he said as he strode out the door.

"Later, Jimmy." Sal was now sitting with the two morose eighth graders, sulking right along with them. Whatever they had was contagious.

I finished my sandwiches, put some money on the bar, said my good-byes, and left. I rode home slowly, running the whole scenario through my head as I pedaled.

Our mystery player "B" wanted Nikki taken out, but didn't necessarily want to get her hands dirty. So first she contacted Joey, an old flame who usually had no problem whacking kids. Except this time he does. It might be too generous to credit Joey with having a moment of clarity. It seems more like an animal instinct for self-preservation. So, in that moment of self-preservation, Joey says he needs some time to think about it, which in his line of work is a way of saying no without actually saying no. It's like your mom saying "we'll see" when you ask her for ice cream after dinner. So as he's thinking about it, "B" sends him a few mementos, hoping to persuade him through his heart. No dice. So "B" goes through with it on her own, but tries awfully hard to pin it on Joey. She was pretty successful. But why did she send the envelope if she was prepared to do it herself? She might have been a little nervous, sure . . . but to leave incriminating evidence seemed sloppy to me. But who was I to say? So far, I was the only one who cared about this case enough to still be working on it. Maybe she had counted on that. She had to know that most kids around here hated Joey and wouldn't care what happened to him. Or maybe she was just sloppy. People are sloppy all the time. The more I thought about the possibilities, the more the answers seemed to slip away.

When I got home I was pooped, but still had some work to do. As I was unlocking my office door, the phone started ringing. I got to it on the fifth ring. It was Kevin.

"What the hell are you doing?" he barked.

"Hello? Who is this?"

"You know damn well who it is. What did you say to Vinny?"

"I told him the truth. I don't think Joey popped Nikki."

"You know how that makes me look?"

"Yeah, like an idiot."

"You don't get it, do you? If Joey didn't do it, I'm screwed."

"Well, whose fault is that? Huh? You're the one who went off half-cocked and took out the wrong kid."

"You have proof?"

"Maybe."

"This isn't a game, Matt!"

"I've got a lead. That's all I'm going to tell you, so you might as well stop asking."

"Bury it."

"What?"

"Bury it. Get rid of it. I know we haven't been the best of friends lately, but we used to be. So please, in the spirit of that . . ."

"This is the second time you've brought up our old friendship. You must really miss me."

"Damn it, Matt, Joey was scum! He may not have deserved it for this hit, but—"

"—he deserved it for others," I finished. "Yeah, I got that memo earlier today. What about justice for Nikki, huh? Or is that not as important as saving your own skin?"

"She's already gone. She can't come back. Don't send me along with her."

"I've gotta go."

"C'mon, Matt! Don't make me do something I don't want to do."

"Are you threatening me?"

"Maybe. Maybe you shouldn't stay awake too long tonight. Your mom might have a later night than usual."

"What? You son of a—" But I was talking to an empty phone line. I yelled at the dead receiver, sputters and grunts and enough curse words to make my principal's head explode. I dialed Kevin's number. The click of the phone being answered was like a sprinter's gun: I heard it and took off

"If you do something to my mom, I swear to God—"

"Matt?" It was Liz on the other line.

"Is Kevin there? I have to talk to him."

"No, he just ran out. What's wrong? What were you saying about—"

"Nothing," I said abruptly. "Forget it."

"Don't snap at me."

"Liz?" a shrill voice called out in the background. "What are you doing on the phone this late?" It was her mother.

"I have to go," Liz said.

"Get off the phone!" the voice cried out. "Now!"

"Just give him the—" I tried to say, but the phone clicked before I could finish. I put the receiver down, sat behind my desk, and stewed. The restaurant was too far away. By the time I got there, whatever was going down would be over. I could call. But what would I say? Pretend I was sick? When my mom got home, then what? *Sorry you didn't make enough money to pay our bills, but I had to fake being sick because Kevin was going to get you in trouble.* That would bring up more problems than it would solve. I would just have to stay awake and wait, like a prisoner in his cell, paying for his crime.

When my mom came in at 4:30 A.M., I was more asleep than awake.

"What happened?" I mumbled.

"Vat of cooking oil fell over in the kitchen, right as we were heading out the door. Total mess," she said, her voice filled with exhaustion. She kissed my forehead and stumbled off to her room.

I wasn't sleepy anymore. I could see Kevin's face in my mind, smirking at me. Two hours later, my alarm was going off. It wasn't going to be a good day.

My mom and I met in the kitchen twenty minutes

later, our eyes barely open. Our conversation consisted of halfhearted grunts, more gorilla than human. Somehow we both managed to get out the door. Halfway to school, I realized that I had forgotten to eat. So the first thing I did when I got there was grab breakfast in the caf. The second thing I did was walk up to Kevin and punch him in the mouth.

"Wake up on the wrong side of the bed this morning, Matt?" he asked, smiling.

I responded with a left jab to the other side of his mouth. He expected the first punch, but not the second. A thin line of blood trickled from the corner of his mouth. He wiped it off with the back of his hand. A small crowd formed around us, encouraging us to continue.

"You *had* to drag her into this," I growled. "She didn't have anything to do with it. It was between you and me."

"And you weren't taking me seriously. I wanted to remind you that you should."

I hit him again, this time on his nose. His eyes teared up. He staggered back a couple of steps, but didn't go down. I lowered my head and charged, driving my right shoulder into his ribs. The back of his head clanged off the lockers. I rebounded off of him, losing my balance a bit.

He didn't hesitate; he put his hand on my face and pushed me over. I fell, but rolled right back to my feet before he could get a shot in. We squared off, each waiting for the other to make a move.

We used to play-fight like this all the time when we were friends, but things never escalated past the "tap and laugh" phase. Kev always held back because I was much smaller than him. At the moment though, playtime was over. There was a really good chance that I was about to get pummeled.

That's when an orange sash caught my eye. A hall monitor was standing there, watching. I was a little relieved—I might get in trouble, but at least I'd still be alive. I waited for the monitor to break us up. Nothing happened. I looked at the monitor more closely. It was Jenny's friend Mel. She was standing in front of the crowd, a little too close to the action, her eyes focused on Kevin's face.

My mind started racing. What was she doing? Why wasn't she breaking up the fight?

Kevin popped me in the chin, reminding me that I had bigger things to worry about at the moment. I wobbled on my feet. Before Kevin got a chance to put me down, a voice intervened from the back of the crowd.

"Break it up! Break it up!" It was Gerry Tinsdale, a seventh-grade hall monitor. Everyone scattered as he walked over, like a flock of birds looking for a new feeder. Mel had melted into the crowd.

Gerry was a runt of a kid. Kevin could have broken him in two, used half of him as a toothpick, and put the other half in his pocket for later. But what Gerry lacked in size he made up for in authority. Break Gerry, and you'd have to answer to Katie Kondo, hall monitor chief. Nobody, not even Kevin, wanted to do that.

"What the hell's going on here?" Gerry demanded in a voice toughened by the sash he wore.

"Nothing," I said.

"Yeah, nothing," Kevin repeated.

"Nothing, huh? Carling, you've got a little . . ." Gerry tapped the corner of his mouth.

Kevin wiped the blood away. "That's weird," he said. "Where'd that come from?"

"Maybe from the fight you two cupcakes were having?" Gerry offered.

"Fight?" Kevin said, with all the innocence of a kid caught with an atlas during a geography test. "Us?"

"No, no, no," I said. "You've got it all wrong."

"We were practicing something for—"

"English class," I said. Kevin looked at me and smiled, then closed his eyes and shook his head slowly back and forth. I smiled back. I couldn't help it. It was a horrible cover story. We'd always had an easy camaraderie. It had never gone away, no matter how many times we'd tried to kill it.

"Cute story, but I'm not here 'cause of your little game of patty-cake. Katie wants to talk to you," Gerry said, pointing at me.

"Me?" I asked. "How come?"

"You'll have to ask her."

"Well, listen, I would love to shoot the breeze with her, but I've got a test in English."

"It'll keep. Let's go. Get to class, Carling."

"Yes, sir!" Kevin said, giving a mock salute. "We'll continue our conversation later, Matt." As he walked away, he shot me a smile that was equal parts amusement and malice.

"C'mon, Stevens," Gerry said. "You don't want to keep Katie waiting."

"How do you know what I want?"

"Call it a hunch."

Katie Kondo was the first seventh grader in the history of Franklin Middle School to ever make hall monitor chief, and she didn't get there by being sweet. She was tough, relentless, and built like a cement wall. You couldn't bribe her. You couldn't threaten her. She had the principal's ear and the weight of the school behind her. If you were guilty, she wouldn't stop until she made you pay. She did everything by the rules, and had no patience for those who couldn't or wouldn't. Consequently, she wasn't my biggest fan.

"Sit down, Stevens," she said as I entered her office. Gerry went behind the desk and whispered something in her ear. "Tell her I want to see her," she responded through gritted teeth. Gerry nodded his head and hustled out of there, like a bobble-head with a jet pack.

"Matt Stevens," Katie said, as if I were a disease that had killed a loved one.

"You know, you're keeping me from a English te—"

"What do you know about Joey Renoni?" she asked, interrupting me.

"Well, he has a lovely singing voice . . ."

"You're not funny, Matt."

"That's your opinion. Why do you want to know?"

"That's on a need-to-know basis."

"I was just about to tell you the same thing."

"Except you don't have the authority to back it up. *I* do. How'd you like detention with Mrs. Macready?"

Mrs. Macready was an ancient teacher who probably taught kids on the *Mayflower.* She put her detention charges to work as if it *were* the 1600s, washing walls and cleaning bathrooms with toothbrushes.

"Detention? On what charge?"

"Withholding information."

"What information?" I asked.

"You tell me."

"You're bluffing."

"Am I? What do you know about Joey Renoni?" she asked again.

"Who says I know anything?"

"Joey's mom chewed out the principal yesterday for half an hour," she said.

"Actually, it was more like ten minutes."

"Somewhere in the middle, Joey mentioned your name. Now why would he do that?"

"He probably wanted me to get his homework for him while he's absent."

"Hardly. Joey's not absent. He's relocating."

I flinched in surprise. Not a lot, but enough.

"Something wrong, Stevens?"

"Yes. He and I were very close." I sniffled as if I were holding back tears. "I'm going to miss him."

"That's very touching. What happened to Joey?"

"No idea. Why didn't you ask him?"

"I did. He wouldn't answer."

"But he said my name."

"He said he was talking to you. The next thing he knew, two guys dragged him off. He says he didn't see their faces."

"What makes you think *I* did?" I asked.

"Stop playing with me, Matt, and answer my questions!" She slammed her open palm on the table. She was serious. If I didn't give her something, she'd eat me for lunch and not leave room for dessert.

"I know why, not who," I said. "Word got around that it was Joey who popped Nikki."

She looked surprised. "Where'd that come from?"

"You're kidding, right? There were forty kids there when Nikki went down. A few of them heard Joey's giggle flee the scene."

"He didn't do it," she said, so matter-of-factly that it jolted me more than the whole palm-smacking-the-table routine.

"How do you know?"

"The Nikki hit went down around ten after three, right?"

"Right."

"Joey was in here from three to three thirty. Gerry hauled him in for pitching pennies on the side of the building."

If there were any lingering doubts about Joey's innocence, they were gone now.

"Who fingered Joey to you?" Katie asked.

"Not saying. My source came forward in spite of himself."

"It could have been an act. He could have been put up to it."

I thought back to my conversation with Steven Beckett, and how hard it was for him to give me what he knew. If he was faking, he deserved an award. "You could be right," I said, "but I doubt it. It seems more likely that whoever did the hit does a fairly good Joey Renoni impression."

She considered it for a second, then gave a slight nod.

"I'll respect the privacy of your source. Just follow up with him." I bristled at her giving me orders, but decided to let it slide. As it was, I was skating on ice as thin as cheesecloth. She looked at me crossly. "I still think you know who did Joey."

"Sorry. No idea. But if I find out, you'll be the first person I tell," I said, squeezing the sincerity out of me like the last bit of toothpaste in the tube.

She scowled at me. "Get out of here. You're late for class." She didn't say it, but I knew she'd be watching me.

As I left Katie's office, Mel brushed past me on her way in. It was in that moment that I remembered why she had looked so familiar to me. We had gone to Ellie together. She was Katie's little sister.

"Hey, Mel," I said.

She shot me a look like she wanted to dance a jig on my gravesite. Before I had a chance to say anything else, she was inside Katie's office, shutting the door behind her. I hung around outside for a minute, just to satisfy my curiosity. Katie helped me by yelling.

"You're a monitor, for Chrissakes! You're supposed to break up fights, not watch them!"

There was some softer conversation that I couldn't

make out, then more of Katie's yelling. "I don't care what you want! Don't think I don't know what's going on, Melanie. Stay the hell away from Carling. Otherwise, I'm going to Dad, and you'll be off to St. Jude's, got it?" St. Jude's was an all-girls school across town, supposedly with yardstick-wielding nuns the size of steamrollers.

"I told you, I don't care! Don't let it happen again!" Katie yelled. "Now get out of my sight."

I took off. Last thing I wanted was to get caught eavesdropping on a Kondo family conversation. Plus, I had all the info I needed. It didn't take a rocket scientist to

figure out why Katie's knickers were in a twist: Her little sister had a crush on Kevin. That would explain the less-than-pleasant look Mel threw my way; I had punched her Prince Charming in the nose. It was kind of funny when I thought about it, the chief's little sister in love with Vinny's right-hand man. It had all the makings of a tragic romance novel, with the added benefit of driving Katie crazy.

It had been a busy morning, and I hadn't even gone to a class yet. I lay low in the hallways until first period was over, then hustled back to my locker. I pulled the surfer girl figurine out of my pocket. I'd been carrying it around for three days. I'd also been yelled at, hauled in, and knocked around, and every one of my leads had dried up and blown away. So much for good luck.

"I'm going to try this on my own for a little while," I said as I put her on the locker shelf.

Her smile seemed to say, "Suit yourself."

Just then, Mac came running up to me, nearly out of breath. "Matt . . . Matt . . ."

"Take it easy," I said.

"Matt . . ."

"We've established who I am. Now take a deep breath before you give yourself a heart attack."

He took my advice, then broke the bad news. "My folks threw everything out."

"No."

"Yeah. They cleaned the garage a couple of months ago. Tossed all my archives."

I looked at the surfer girl. She smiled as if to say, "Told you so."

"Shut up," I said as I closed my locker door. I looked at Mac to see if he had heard me, but he was in his own world.

"Five years of work, gone. I mean some of it, especially the early stuff, wasn't worth keeping, but some of the later stuff, when I started finding my voice, getting into a groove . . ."

"Who else would have that issue of the paper?"

"I don't know. Could be anyone that was in Ellie at that time. People save all sorts of stuff."

"What other stories ran that week?"

"Oh, geez, Matt . . . that was, like, two years ago."

"Well, think. Whoever else had a story in that paper might have saved it, or had a parent who did."

"Makes sense. You want me to ask around?"

"You want the story?"

"I'll ask around," he said. "Come by my office during lunch."

"Yeah, okay," I said, but he was already gone, weaving through the crowd. I took two steps before Liz Carling stopped me. At this rate, it was going to take me five years to get to class.

"I'm sorry about the whole phone thing last night," she said.

"Okay."

"Aren't you going to say you're sorry, too?"

"Don't push it, Liz." It pained me to see the hurt expression on her face, but I had run out of patience for the Carling family. "Don't you have to get to class or something?"

She ignored me. "Tell me what's going on. Kevin's been out of his mind since what happened to Nikki." She said the name as if it tasted horrible in her mouth.

"You don't want to know."

"Don't tell me what I want or don't want." She tensed her jaw like a boxer ready for the fight to start.

"Go ask your brother. Ask him about the Hyena."

"Joey Renoni? What about him?"

"It was Kevin who had him fitted for a diaper."

It took a moment to sink in. "I don't believe you," she said.

"You don't have to. Ask him. Find out for yourself."

I could tell from her face that she wouldn't need to ask. She knew what her brother was capable of. "He still likes Nikki," was all she could manage. "She's a monster, and he still likes her."

"She's not a monster anymore."

"She'll always be a monster."

"By that definition, so will Kevin."

She sighed and bowed her head as if she couldn't carry the weight of that fact. Kevin and Nikki were in the same business; to love one but hate the other was crazy. "Matt, I'm sorry . . . I—" The bell rang, disrupting her train of thought. She raised her head and looked at me with moist eyes. When the bell stopped ringing, she paused, unsure if she could pick up where she left off.

"What?" I prodded gently. "C'mon Liz. We go way back. If you need to get something off your chest, you can trust me."

She sniffed back some tears and let out a deep sigh. She reached out and touched my arm. Both of us felt the spark. "I—"

Just then, Jenny Finnegan bounded over and wrapped her arms around me. "Matt! You're okay!"

Liz pulled her hand away and closed her mouth before any other words could escape. Jenny let go of me long enough to notice Liz standing there. "Oh. Liz. I . . . I'm sorry. I didn't see you."

"S'okay," she said, barely above a whisper, "I have to get to class."

"Liz," I said, a plaintive note in my voice.

"We'll talk later. We won't have a choice." I was confused, but she just turned and walked to her class.

"I'm sorry, Matt," Jenny said. "I was just so worried about you. I mean, Kevin is huge. When I think of what he could have done to you . . ." She and her ponytail shook at the thought.

"It's all right. He and I have been playing this game for quite a while, and nobody's gotten hurt yet."

"There's always a first time."

"Not always," I said.

"I wish you didn't have to take so many chances," she said.

"It's part of my job."

"The job I gave you."

"You and Vinny."

She winced, as if she didn't like being reminded that Vinny existed. "Quit," she said.

"What?"

"Quit. Right now. Just forget about it. In a lot of ways, Nicole deserved what she got. I love her, but . . ." It was as if she couldn't think of a good way to end that thought. "If something happened to you, I wouldn't . . . I just . . ."

"It wouldn't be your fault," I said, finishing the thought for her. "It would be mine. It would mean I got careless."

"But . . ."

"I'm not quitting, Jenny. I couldn't, even if I wanted to. It's part of what makes me so charming. Plus, I have to make sure I give you your money's worth."

"But I haven't paid you yet."

"Oh. Well, forget it, then. I quit."

She smiled in a way that mixed sadness and gratitude.

"I'm glad I hired you," she said, then kissed me on the cheek, lingering a little. The faint smell of strawberry lip gloss tickled my nose. She pulled a piece of purple stationery out of her bag and wrote down her name and phone number. I smiled. The purple paper had a picture of a horse at the top. "If you need to talk," she said as she placed the paper in my hand. Then she gave me that same half-sad, half-grateful smile, and walked away.

I watched her leave, not sure of what I was feeling. The bell rang. I hustled to English, where we were studying *Romeo and Juliet.* It was a powerful reminder that not every story has a happy ending.

At lunch, I grabbed a quick sandwich, then headed down to Jimmy Mac's. His office was just a small room off the gymnasium. It used to be a closet for gym equipment, but a couple of years ago the school board approved money for a new outdoor storage structure. They moved all the gym stuff out and Jimmy moved in. It was a small room made smaller by the stacks of old newspapers around the room, as if Jimmy had started to build a maze but gave up before finishing. It was the perfect room to cure someone's claustrophobia.

When I walked in, Mac was in the process of making a

bad situation worse. He was moving stacks of papers around without really having a place to put them, like trying to dig a hole in the snow in the middle of an avalanche.

"What are you doing?" I asked.

"Looking for the picture. What do you think?"

I couldn't answer that question, so I let it go. "I thought you were going to ask around," I said.

"I did. Nothing. Every kid who was in that issue cut their story out, then trashed the rest."

"Yeah. Unfortunately, that makes sense. So you think you've got one lying around here?"

"Maybe. When I got this office, I brought over some of my stuff from Ellie, to remind me of my roots, you know? I could swear there was a copy in one of those boxes . . . ," he said.

"Practically at your fingertips . . ."

"What's that?"

"Nothing. Keep looking."

I wondered for a second if the fire inspector knew about this room.

"Hold on a second!" I heard him exclaim in a voice muffled by the mountains of paper between him and me. "Wait . . . wait . . . got it!"

Mac stumbled out from behind a stack and managed to knock over two piles of newspapers. He was clutching a file folder packed beyond capacity. It was labeled *The Elementary Times.* When he opened it, the papers inside fell to the ground, adding to the mess.

"Oh, man," he said, crouching down to pick them up.

I crouched down with him and started sifting. Looking through those newspapers was like pressing fast forward on the development of Jimmy's life. You could tell the first-grade ones with a glance, their crude writing and pictures glaring back at you like art from a refrigerator door. The papers stopped at third grade; fourth and fifth weren't there. Jimmy Mac noticed it, too. "Fifth's not here?" he asked. "Oh, man . . ." We both stared at the piles of papers scattered around us. Trying to find the photo in that mess was going to be like trying to find a grain of salt on a sandy beach.

"I'll come back later," I said, standing up.

"Yeah. I'll need a few minutes." Another pile of papers fell over, as if on cue.

"Or a few days," I said. "You know, you should really get—"

"A filing cabinet. Yeah, I know, I know . . ." Jimmy disappeared behind a couple of stacks, shuffling sounds the only evidence that he was still in the room. I left just as the bell rang.

As I walked to class, I passed Mel in the hallway. She looked stiff and unnatural in her monitor sash. She saw me coming and scowled. Usually, I'd let it go, but right now wasn't usually. "Hey!" I shouted. She came to an abrupt stop, then took a couple of shuffling steps forward, as if she wasn't sure I was talking to her. I wanted to make her sure. "Melanie. You're Katie's sister, right?"

"Yeah?" she said, turning toward me. On her list of things to do in life, it looked like talking to me was right below being eaten by sharks.

"Well, listen, if you're mad at me because of that fight with Kevin—"

Some air escaped through her clenched teeth, loud enough to cut me off. She sounded like an overheated radiator trying to let off some steam before it exploded. When she spoke, each word dripped with hatred: "Don't . . . talk . . . to . . . me!" The last word came out like an angry shriek. Kids in the hallway stopped to see what was going on. Melanie didn't wait for my reaction;

she just turned and stomped off. I was probably off her Christmas card list.

After Algebra, I went to the hall pay phone and called Joey to see if I could get some info about that photo. I hung up when the Renoni family answering machine picked up. I was barely prepared to talk to Joey; I had no idea what to say to Joey's answering machine. As I let go of the receiver, a hand the size of a canned ham grabbed my wrist and turned me around. The other ham hand grabbed the front of my shirt, making me glad I didn't have any chest hair yet. The enormous kid attached to those hands lifted me off the ground, slamming my back into the wall. It was one of Vinny's bodyguards.

"Hello, Matthew," Vinny said, walking up beside me. I was able to look down on him since my feet were dangling a foot off the floor.

"Hello, Vincent. To what do I owe the pleasure?"

"I was just telling Andrew here how coincidental it was that we should run across you on the phone, since that's precisely why I wanted to speak with you."

"I'm assuming this Neanderthal is Andrew."

Andrew shook me a couple of times to assure me that he was.

"Andrew here suggested smashing your head against this wall to teach you a lesson about proper phone etiquette," Vinny said. "Insult him again, and I'll take his suggestion."

"Fine. You proved your point."

"I'm not sure I have yet. There are certain aspects of my business that I would rather not discuss over the phone. A smart kid like you should be able to figure out what those things are. If you can't, Andrew here can help you. Any time, any place. Are we clear?"

"Crystal. Now put me down."

Andrew looked at Vinny, who gave him a subtle nod. Andrew put me back on the ground. I smoothed out the front of my shirt, rubbing a spot on my shoulder that was going to be sore later. I shot Andrew a dirty look. He snickered.

"Now," Vinny said, "I believe you had a question about hall passes?"

"Maybe."

Vinny laughed. "Yes, well, I personally don't have any experience with them—"

"No, of course not."

"But a friend of mine has. Last year, this friend of

mine used to get things like that from an eighth-grade boy, I believe his name was Charlie something. Anyway, when Charlie graduated, it left a sizable hole in my friend's business."

"Couldn't Charlie do them from high school?"

"Apparently not. Charlie made it clear that he didn't have time for things like that anymore."

"Makes you wonder what goes on in high school."

"Indeed. Anyway, a couple of days later, someone got in touch with my friend about providing such a service."

"How?"

"Anonymous note left in his locker. There was an offer and a set of explicit instructions."

"Does he still have that note?" I asked.

"He doesn't keep things like that."

"Not even for his scrapbook?"

"Anyway, the note instructed him to leave money on the top shelf of his locker at the start of the day. Then take all the books he needed until after lunch and lock the locker as he normally would. He couldn't go back to his locker until after lunch. If he did, the deal was off."

"And your friend trusted this person?"

"Of course not. But my friend doesn't keep anything

in his locker other than his school books. It's the first place they check."

"Who's 'they'—the principal or the FBI?"

He ignored the question. "And he figured, what the heck? He can try it once, just to see what happens. He can always find out later who's behind it if he wants."

"Right."

"So, he leaves the money, locks his locker, then spends the day B.A.U."

"B.A.U.?"

"Business as usual. When he goes back to his locker, the money is gone. In its place, an envelope. In the envelope, a stack of hall passes."

"How many?"

"However many he paid for."

"Thanks for being specific. How'd the forger get into his locker?"

"No idea."

"Your friend didn't think to stake it out?"

"Of course he did. A week later, he received another note, same instructions. He went through the same routine, but this time, one of his associates watched the locker the entire morning. She stayed out of sight, never taking her eyes off it. There was no way the forger would have time to complete the transaction without being seen, even in the hustle and bustle of the normal, everyday hallway.

"Two periods passed with no action. After the third-period bell, the hallway filled up with kids, as per usual. When the hallway cleared out, there was a bright orange sticky note on the outside of the locker door. My friend's associate knew she had been spotted. She came out of her hiding spot and grabbed the note. It said 'If you continue to watch, there'll be nothing to see . . . ever again.' The knowledge of who was writing the passes was much less valuable than the actual passes, so my friend decided: no more stakeouts."

"You didn't try to ask around? Try to get some info on the forger?"

"As I just said, *my friend* saw the value in the passes themselves, not in the kid who wrote them. When faced with the choice, he chose to keep the business relationship intact, and keep the forger's identity secret."

"That seems a little out of character for your *friend*."

"You have no idea about the character of my friend," Vinny said. I wasn't sure I believed him. Vinny wasn't the kind of kid who would have a sizable part of his business reliant on a mystery person. "Now then, Matthew, anything else?" he asked. It was his way of closing the subject. I could press on, but at my own risk. I decided to switch gears.

"Yeah, couple of things. First, Kevin—"

"Has been talked to. He was understandably concerned about your investigation. He has been assured that his place in the organization is secure."

"Awfully sporting of you."

Vinny shrugged. "What's done is done. Joey may not have deserved it for Nicole—"

"But he deserved it for others. So that's the company line, huh?"

"It's even simpler than that. Joey is gone. Kevin still has value to the organization. He isn't going anywhere. He just needed a little assurance."

"Nice boss."

"Don't sound so surprised. Anything else?"

I pulled out the half photo of Joey and handed it to Vinny. "Recognize this?"

Vinny studied it without giving an indication either way. "Should I?"

"It's half of a newspaper photo. It was taken at Spring Fling back in fifth. I need the other half."

"Check with—"

"Jimmy Mac? Already did. He's looking through his archives, but his filing system leaves a lot to be desired. Here." I handed him the note signed "B." "Do you know if Joey was seeing a girl whose name had a 'B' in it?"

Vinny laughed. "You're kidding, right? Without even trying, I can think of two dozen 'B' girls that Joey dated. If I try, I can think of four dozen."

"Yeah, I heard Joey had a following."

The bell rang.

"Sorry," Vinny said, handing me back the papers, "you're on your own. I'll check in with you later, to make sure I'm getting my money's worth. Andrew."

Andrew gave me a casual pat on the arm that almost dislocated my shoulder. I watched them walk away. Katie Kondo sidled up, trying to sneak up on me, but she made more noise than an elephant in tap shoes.

"Have a nice chat with Vinny?" she asked.

"Yes, in fact. He's a great conversationalist."

"Got something you want to confess?"

"Yes. Yes, I do. I love you, Katie. I always have, and I

always will. You . . . ," I sighed for dramatic effect, ". . . complete me."

Katie scowled at me. "What did you talk about?"

"Nothing much. You know, sports, the weather, the fall TV schedule . . ."

"I thought you were going to help me, Matt."

"And I thought you were going to stay out of my business, Katie."

"Not when your business and mine are the same thing."

"You know, that's why I could never work for you. You're too hands-on. People see you coming and they just clam up. How do you get any info that way?"

"By shaking down the likes of you. One word from me, Stevens, and you're out of business. Don't forget that."

"Listen, just because you're upset with your sister, don't take it out on me."

"What?" She went from annoyed to furious in a split second.

"Nothing, never mind . . . Forget I said—" Katie cut me off with a punch to the stomach. The only reason I didn't fall to my knees was because I had the wall to lean back on. She stood over me, fists poised to hit me again.

"Don't *ever* talk about my sister," she hissed. "Don't even think her name. She's got a bright future ahead of her, and you and your type are not going to ruin it. Got it?" She didn't wait for an answer. She stormed through the hallway, kids scattering out of her path. I leaned there for a minute, trying to catch my breath. Punches like that made you wonder if the guy who thought up the expression "hits like a girl" had ever met one.

I was still rubbing my stomach a couple of hours later when I stopped at my locker. Katie's punch was the gift that kept on giving. I grabbed my books, anxious to scram and put this school day behind me, when I saw a note on the top shelf, next to the surfer girl, whose smile was now openly mocking me.

It was from Liz. "We need to talk. I'll call you later." The thought of Liz calling me for any reason was enough to make the pain in my stomach subside a little. It came back when I remembered our previous conversation. Liz had something to tell me, and it hadn't sounded like a good thing. Our talk tonight would most likely be the cherry on top of my crap sundae of a day.

When I got home, my mom's car was in the driveway.

It was the kind of car that made you wonder how quickly they fired the team that designed it. She was supposed to be at the restaurant, which meant that the car had broken down again, stranding my mom and putting even more stress on our already thin finances. I walked into the kitchen expecting the worst, but I was in for a pleasant surprise: My mom was sitting at the table with a big smile on her face.

"What's wrong with the car?" I asked, even though I knew by my mom's expression that the car was fine.

"Nothing. Things were slow at the restaurant so Mr. Carling gave me the night off," she said excitedly.

"What's in it for him?" I asked.

"You know what? Tonight, I couldn't care less. What say you and me go grab a sandwich downtown?"

I furrowed my brow at her, silently asking her whether we should spend the money. It was a knee-jerk reaction. My mom looked sad that her son was being raised to worry like that, but her enthusiasm was not going to be squashed.

"I found a little extra money . . . ," she said.

I smiled broadly, knowing where that money actually came from. Whatever animosity I felt toward Vinny evaporated. I was sure I'd find some more soon, but at that moment, I wished him good tidings and an endless supply of snack cakes.

"Let me just change my shoes," Mom said, and ran into her room. I heard my phone ringing downstairs. Liz. I started for the cellar door, my heart beating like a jackrabbit's. As my hand hit the doorknob, my mom came out of her room.

"Where are you going?" she asked.

"Nowhere. The phone downstairs was ringing. I was just going to go pick it up. Let the person know they had the wrong number."

My mom gave me a kiss on the forehead. "You're so considerate, but let it ring. Just for tonight, let's be a little selfish."

I buried my disappointment in the biggest smile I could muster. "Sounds good, Mom." We walked out the door. The phone kept ringing, the answers to some of my questions waiting for me on the other end. They would have to keep 'til tomorrow.

The downtown area had a boardwalk along the river lined with stores and restaurants. My mom and dad and I had spent hours walking there when he was still in the picture. My parents loved to window-shop, looking at all the things they'd buy if they just had a little extra money.

When my father disappeared, my mother and I didn't come down here as much. It was just too painful, like going back to the scene of a crime. As the years passed and some of the pain subsided, our viewpoint began to change. It began to feel like a scrapbook you could walk through.

My mom and I stopped at Lucy's, our favorite sandwich place. It was an old hole-in-the-wall—a relic of the town's rougher past. They had the biggest and best sandwiches around. Paulie, a tough, old ex-Navy man, was behind the counter, putting sandwiches together. He was grumpy to everyone, except my mom. He had an obvious soft spot for her. She had that effect on people.

"Hey, Kathy. What can I get you?" he asked.

"Hmm . . ." My mom always took her time, even though she always ended up ordering the same thing. "I think I'll have a cheesesteak with onions and mushrooms."

"You got it. What do you want, kid? C'mon. I ain't got all night."

"Can I get the chicken Parm?"

He huffed and rolled his eyes as if I'd ordered lobster thermidor. He turned around and started cooking. My mom and I sat down in the molded plastic seats that were as uncomfortable as they looked. She absentmindedly picked up a brochure of houses for sale, none of which we could afford. "So, how's school?" she asked. It was her go-to question.

"Okay," I said, and shrugged. My mom looked at me

with a mixture of suspicion and amusement. "What?" I asked.

Before she could answer, Paulie yelled, "Order up!" and put our bag of sandwiches on the counter. "I threw in some French fries, on the house," he said. "You need to put some meat on those bones."

My mother smiled a shy little smile. "Thanks, Paulie. What would I do without you?"

"You'd starve."

We paid and left. We sat down outside on one of the park benches overlooking the river. It was a little cooler sitting by the water. We sat there for a while, quietly eating our sandwiches. My mom finally broke the silence. "You think about him a lot in the fall."

I nodded and bit into my chicken Parm. It had been my dad's favorite.

It'd been more than six years since he disappeared. He went to work one Thursday morning and never came home. My mom did all the things you're supposed to do. She went to the police. When forty-eight hours had passed and we hadn't heard from him, she'd filed a missing persons report. She cried, a lot. Nothing worked. He stayed gone.

Five days later, the police found our car in a parking

garage four states away. They also found the note in the glove compartment: TMS136P15, neatly typed in the left corner of an otherwise blank sheet of paper. Nobody had any idea what it meant, or if it was even a clue. When the police told my mom, she said she had no idea what it was. Even at six years old, I noticed there was something different about her from that point on. She stopped crying. She took down a lot of the photos of my dad. We moved out of the place they had shared since before I was born, and into the apartment that we live in now. I've asked my mom more than a few times what that series of letters and numbers meant, but she's always denied knowing. Finally, I stopped asking. My mom may know what it means, but she's made it perfectly clear that she's not going to tell me. The only thing I was doing by continuing to bring it up was making her feel bad. I decided to try to figure it out for myself.

I've looked at all the police reports, the ones that I've had access to. I've pored over the photographs. I even got a chance to question the investigating officer. Nothing. I wish I could pursue some other leads, but it's tough. They found the car four states away, and my only means of transportation is a bike. When I turn sixteen, I know the first place I'm driving to, but by then the case will be ten years old, and colder than an Alaskan winter. My dad could have been kidnapped. He could be living in California under an assumed name. He could be touring around the universe in a spaceship, or living with Amelia Earhart on a desert island. Any of these seem possible.

"You never answered my question from before," my mom said, pulling me back into the present.

"What question?"

"How's school?"

"I did too answer it. I said it's okay."

"What'd you do today?"

"Nothing."

"Hmm. So it's going okay, and you did nothing. Great answer."

I shrugged. What was I going to tell her? *I had a great day at school today, except I can't seem to make any headway in this case I'm working on. You see, someone soaked the front of Nikki Fingers's pants. Oh, and someone put Joey Renoni in a diaper, then covered the back of it with chocolate, but everybody thinks it's something else, if you get my drift. Don't know who Nikki Fingers and Joey Renoni are? Oh, well let me describe Vinny Biggs's whole criminal operation.* It made a discussion with her about sex seem easy by comparison.

"Don't you want to know how my day was?" she asked.

"Sure," I said, relieved by the change of subject.

"It was okay."

"Oh yeah?" I said, playing along. "What'd you do today?"

"Nuthin'" she said, as if her IQ had just dropped fifty points.

We looked at each other and laughed. When the laughter trailed off, she started in again. "You got something on your mind?" she asked.

"What? No."

"Matthew, if you want to keep secrets, you're going to have to work on your facial expressions. Now spill it. Pretend for a moment you're not outgrowing your mom."

I knew I wasn't going to be able to get off the hook without giving her something to chew on. There's nothing more persistent than a concerned mother. They're like rottweilers with good intentions. Even though I hated to resort to clichés, I knew there was one phrase that every adult expects to hear when a guy is having trouble. "Well, there's this girl at school—"

"Mm-hmm," my mom said with a knowing smile. "I figured."

I smiled back, hoping that she read it as slight embarrassment instead of mild triumph. She had taken the bait.

"Does she like you?" she asked.

"I don't know. Sometimes it seems like she does. Then, other times it seems like she hates me."

"Are you nice to her?"

"Sometimes. But sometimes I'm mean to her, and I just can't help it."

"Hmm."

"Then there's this other girl who seems to like me a lot, but I'm not sure how I feel about her. Sometimes when I'm with her, I think that we could be happy together, and I can forget all about girl number one. But then I see girl number one again . . ."

"And you feel something that just isn't there with girl number two, no matter how much you want it to be."

"Yeah." An uncomfortable realization hit me: I was no longer making up a story—I was actually talking about what was going on between Liz, Jenny, and me. Somehow, my mom had gotten me to open up about what was really going on in my life. She was like a human truth serum. I had to be careful. Giving my mom too much info could make it difficult for me to operate.

"I know, Matt. Trust me . . . I know. It isn't easy. You're torn, right?"

I carefully nodded yes.

"You think that, yeah, there may be a couple of things that you're concerned about with girl number one, but there's no denying how you feel. You need to see her every day, because if you don't, you feel like there's something missing, something very important that you forgot to do. And those things that you're concerned about, those are just problems to tackle together, things that can be worked out. But you're not sure, because the problems you have with her seem pretty big, and you don't know if they can be solved."

I nodded again.

"Girl number two, however, is an open book," she said. "She seems honest and straightforward. She makes her feelings known, and when you're with her, you think to yourself, 'This is easy. It's so hard with girl number one. It shouldn't be that hard. Maybe I should forget her and go for girl number two.' The only problem is that, although you like girl number two, you're not sure if you *like her* like her. And you wonder, if you decide to go with girl number two, and girl number one comes around, what the heck will you do then?"

"Yeah," I said. I felt a little naked. My mom had taken a chunk of my brain and read it whole, like a book she picked up at the library. What else did she know about me?

"Yeah, Matt, I know how you feel. I think everyone goes through something like that at least once in their lives."

"So what do I do?" The question slipped out before I had a chance to stop it.

"No idea."

"Oh."

"Matt, you're going to have regrets no matter what you choose. You'll always have a part of you that wonders, 'What if I had made the other choice?' But that's true with any choice you have to make. The only thing you can do is choose and hope for the best. Trust me. I speak from experience." She took a bite of her sandwich.

I tried to guess the experience she was talking about, but I had no idea. I knew very little about her past, mostly because she never talked about it. There were a few old photos of her family in our apartment, but she never let family become a topic of discussion. I knew she had a sister, out west somewhere, I think, but we never saw or heard from her. I knew nothing about my grandparents, other than that both sets were dead. Her life before me was a mystery, one that I hardly ever asked about. When we finally did get to spend time together, the last thing I wanted to do was bring up a tough subject.

"I know you were looking for a more concrete answer," she said, "but I think you're old enough to realize that sometimes there isn't one."

"I appreciate the honesty."

"Thought you might."

"No matter how unhelpful it is," I said, smiling.

"What? You want your mommy to solve all your problems?" she said, smiling back.

"Only the hard ones."

"Sorry, kiddo. You're in the deep end of the pool now, and I already have a pretty good idea of how strong a swimmer you are."

"What do you mean?" I asked.

She paused, her eyes never leaving mine. "I want a hot chocolate. You?"

"Sure," I replied, more than a little confused by her swimmer comment.

"This time, we'll use *my* money." Before I could respond, she crumpled up her empty sandwich wrapper, stood up, and started walking away. She knew about my little contribution to her emergency fund. I wondered again how much my mom really knew about the life I led.

"Well?" she asked, turning toward me. "You coming?"

I stood up and threw my trash in a nearby garbage can—the fancy wrought-iron kind that let people know the town had money. We walked toward the coffee shop that was just about to close. My mom looked in the windows of the stores as we passed. We held hands, but didn't say anything.

When we got home that night, it was 9:30. I knew calling Liz that late would be a disaster, but I wanted to anyway. I talked myself out of it. Waiting until the next day shouldn't be too hard. By 3:30 in the morning, I almost had myself convinced. Around 4:00, I finally drifted off into a restless sleep.

I dreamed that I was in school, walking to my locker. The front of my pants was soaked. The hallway was full of kids, all of them pointing and laughing at me. When I got to my locker, I couldn't remember the combination. I kept spinning the dial, like a carnie working the Wheel of Fortune. The crowd kept growing behind me, their laughter growing with them. Liz walked up to me, but it wasn't just Liz; she was a combination of Liz, Jenny, and Nikki Fingers. "Matt, I really need to tell you something," she said, as if she didn't see the situation around me. I looked at her with wide, hopeful eyes. Maybe she didn't see what was going on. Maybe I could salvage this. As I opened my mouth to say something, this Liz-Jenny-Nikki girl slowly raised a squirt gun, one the size of a fire hose. She was crying, crying and pumping her squirt gun, building up pressure for a maximum blast. "I'm sorry, Matt," she said, "but this is the way it has to be." She turned the gun on me. Its nozzle looked as big as a tunnel, as black as a storm cloud.

I woke up right as she pulled the trigger. I was breathing heavy, drenched in sweat; for a second I thought I *had* been soaked with a squirt gun. But then I blinked away the sleep and recognized my room. I breathed a sigh of relief and untangled the covers that had become twisted around me like a makeshift toga. I looked at the clock on my nightstand. The nightmare had seemingly lasted for hours. In actual time, it was only forty-five minutes.

It was 4:45. I had to wait at least fifteen minutes before

getting up. Waking up at 5:00 means you're industrious, an early riser; waking up at 4:45 means you have trouble sleeping.

As I waited, the unexpected happened: I drifted off into a smooth, dreamless sleep. When the alarm woke me up at 6:30, I couldn't believe that an hour and a half had passed. Time is elastic, shrinking and expanding in certain situations. It loves to sneak past you when you aren't paying attention, and slow to a crawl when you are.

When I dragged myself out of bed to turn off the alarm, my head felt like it was filled with cotton, like a cheap stuffed animal. I had a tired taste in my mouth. I staggered out into the kitchen to grab some juice. On the counter was a note from my mom. It said: "Hi honey, Hope you have an okay day doin' nuthin'. Love, Mom." I smiled. No more underestimating her.

I showered, grabbed a quick breakfast, and headed off to school. The chill autumn air cleared my head a little, like a cup of coffee I could breathe. In the course of trying to forget my dream and get out the door that morning, I had forgotten that Liz wanted to talk to me. I remembered it now, full force. The tingle in my stomach worked its way up into my chest, nearly completing the job that the brisk air had started. I was almost awake now, despite the lack of sleep, and the pace of my walk quickened.

My mind drifted back to the first moment I realized there might be something between Liz and me. One fall day a couple of years ago, I had biked over to the Carling house to see if Kevin was around and up for doing something. Liz answered the door and told me that Kevin had gone off with their father on some errand. I was disappointed. I had no idea how I was going to spend the rest of my day.

"I don't have anything going on," I remember Liz saying.

I initially dismissed the idea of hanging out with Liz all day. Then, since the prospect of spending the day alone didn't thrill me, I thought, *What the hell?* It might still be the best decision I ever made. We wandered around town, talking effortlessly for hours, about everything and nothing at all. There were no weird pauses or uncomfortable silences, just an endless stream of conversation. When it was finally time to go home, neither of us wanted to. We had spent six hours together. I got the feeling that we could have spent six hundred hours together and we would have felt the same way: We didn't want to leave each other.

From that day forward I started to think more and more about Liz, my feelings for her, and what it all meant. I started to think that she might be my best friend, not Kevin. Then other possibilities started popping into my head. What if Liz was more than just a friend? I had no idea what to think about that, and even less of an idea what she thought about it.

That's the frustrating thing about girls . . . You finally figure out how you feel about one of them, and then you have to figure out how they feel about you. Couldn't girls just send out a signal or something? Maybe they could have an "I like you" stick that they hit you with, or a big neon sign they could place over their heads that tells you "yes" or "no." All I know is that there has to be a better system than the one we're stuck with.

When I got to school, I was a little disappointed that Liz wasn't in front waiting for me. I laughed at my unrealistic expectations. When I got to my locker, and Liz wasn't there, either, I went through the same cycle. I tried to convince myself that I would talk to Liz when the time was right, but as soon as I heard footsteps behind me, I almost sprained my neck turning around.

"Hey!" I said, a little too quickly and a lot too loud.

"Hey, yourself!" Jenny said, matching my enthusiasm. I masked my disappointment. I didn't want her to feel bad.

"What's up?"

"I called you last night, but nobody picked up."

"I was out late," I said.

"Oh." I could tell that she wanted to ask me more questions, like "Where?" or "With who?" I turned away from her, toward my locker, before she had the chance. Being out with my mom wasn't exactly great for my business image.

As I opened my locker, there was a strange *riki-tik-tik* sound. Part of brain was yelling at me, warning me that something was wrong, but I was tired, and when you're tired, you tend to overlook small details. The *riki-tik-tik* sound increased as I opened the locker door wider.

"Look out!" Jenny yelled, pushing me out of the way. Something flew past, hitting the wall behind me with a splat. The strong aroma of cat urine filled the hallway. Kids stopped, trying to figure out what the heck had just happened. I was right there with them.

Jenny was lying on top of me. "Are you okay, Matt?" she asked, still panting. I nodded yes, but I wasn't sure yet. She climbed off me and gave me a hand getting up.

"Booby trap," she said between heavy breaths.

I looked in my locker. A large elastic band hung inside like overcooked spaghetti. One end of it had been attached to my locker door; the other end attached to the back of my locker with a paper clip. A slingshot for a urine-filled balloon. When the paper clip bent, it fired the balloon at where my crotch would have been . . . if Jenny hadn't pushed me out of the way.

"How did you know?" I asked Jenny.

"The sound," she said, still out of breath. "My sister . . ." She took a deep breath and started over: "My sister used to make them all the time. I remember her testing them in our basement. The balance between the elastic and the paper clip had to be just right, otherwise it wouldn't work. She'd test it for hours. The best elastics made that that *riki-tik* sound as they were pulled tight. I haven't heard it in so long . . . It was a technique she was pretty proud of."

I wondered again why I was trying to find justice for Nicole, a girl who once took great pleasure in devising traps like this. The case had started out as a pure money deal, but no job I've ever taken was only about the money. I knew that my pride and ego were wrapped up in it, but I liked to think I had some altruistic motives, too, even if I had a hard time coming up with any at that moment. Before the question derailed me, I had a flash of intuition. One glance at the top shelf in my locker confirmed that I was right. My "good luck charm" was gone. "They stole the little surfer girl," I said.

"No!"

I was upset, mostly because I wanted to yell "I told you so!" into the face of that little surfer girl; I didn't need her "good luck" to escape the Outs. I guess that made me a couple of pins short of the spare. Before I checked into the loony bin, I figured I should start being the detective I claimed to be. "Who did your sister teach her technique to?" I asked Jenny.

"The assassins," she said. "All of them."

"How many is that?"

"I think around thirty."

"Great. Only thirty?"

"But who knows who they taught."

"Right. Thanks." Someday, I'd have to introduce Jenny to sarcasm.

"Oh, my god, what time is it?" she asked.

I looked at the clock in the hallway. It was 7:45. I said so.

"I have to go." She ran off in a full sprint. I grabbed my first-period textbook, spared one last moment to look at the booby trap that almost ended my life, then took off after her. A crowd of kids were gathering around the cat pee splat, like snobs in a gallery admiring an artist's latest work.

I almost lost sight of Jenny, but then found her again. She was taking a path that was easily identifiable to me: She was headed for the principal's office.

When she was a few steps away, the door to the office opened, almost as if on cue. It seemed to play out in slow motion. Jenny kept running toward the door. The principal came walking out with a plain-looking girl in baggy clothes. For a moment, I wondered if it was Jenny's cousin—a girl who shared the family features, but who I had never seen before. It was only after a minute that I realized that the girl coming out of the principal's office was actually Nicole Finnegan. Apparently, everyone in the hallway realized it at the same time I did, because all movement and discussion stopped, as if someone had pressed the pause button on a remote control.

Nicole had gone through a drastic transformation over the past couple of days. She looked haggard and washed out. Her hair, which used to be the shimmering auburn of fall leaves, was now a dull, burnt umber color. Her skin used to look smooth and white, like a freshly opened container of cream cheese. Now it was pale and clammy. Her eyes, bloodshot and puffy from crying, darted from face to face. She expected the inevitable ridicule from the crowd, and she was afraid.

Nicole passed through the hallway, leaving a trail of whispers and barely contained laughter. The crowd held off because of the presence of the principal, but you could feel the pressure building. Jenny followed close by, and I caught her eye as she passed. She looked resigned, as if she knew she'd be spending the rest of the year shepherding her sister around school. "Talk to you later," she said in a voice usually reserved for funerals. I nodded solemnly, with respect for the departed.

Throughout the day, I caught glimpses of Jenny as she ushered Nicole to her classes. Jenny tried to defend her sister against the laughter and taunts of her classmates, but Nikki had made too many enemies. She had brought a lot of misery to a lot of kids at the Frank. Finally, her bill had come, and her classmates were going to make sure she paid every last cent of it.

By the time lunch rolled around, Jenny and Nicole looked beaten down, exhausted by the constant barrage of insults from all sides. They had different lunch periods. Nicole went first. Jenny walked her to the cafeteria doors, stopping at the entrance. Nicole walked forward as if the floor were coated in ice. She kept looking back at Jenny, her face full of fear and sadness, like a preschooler leaving her mom behind and getting on the school bus for the first time.

When Nicole walked in, all activity in the caf stopped. She turned to Jenny, a look of panic in her eyes. Jenny couldn't make up her mind whether to whisk her sister out of there or let it ride and hope for the best. A passing teacher made up her mind for her. "Get to class, Miss Finnegan." When Jenny didn't move right away, the teacher stopped and looked back at her. "Now!" Jenny sighed, gave her sister one last encouraging look, and walked off.

Nicole stood frozen, watching her sister leave. As soon as Jenny was out of view, an open carton of chocolate milk flew out of nowhere and struck Nicole in the side of the head. Chocolate milk dripped down her face and hair like muddy water. The caf erupted in cheers and laughter. Nicole started to cry.

As she turned to face her attackers, another carton of milk came flying toward her head. She made no move to avoid it; she just hung her head and closed her eyes, bracing herself for impact, tears and chocolate milk forming a puddle around her feet. When the impact didn't happen, she opened her eyes in surprise. She looked around to see what had happened. I was what had happened.

I had caught the carton before it hit her. I hated mob scenes, ever since a freeze-tag incident from a couple of years ago. And after the morning I'd had, I was damned if I was going to let a mob ruin my lunch.

The crowd quieted down; I had their attention, but not for long. "Thanks for the free milk," I said. I opened it up and took a sip. A few kids in the crowd laughed. For a second, I thought I had ended the incident before it really had a chance to get ugly. I almost didn't see the kid a few feet away from me readying his mashed-potato spoon-catapult, with Nicole dead in his sights. I hooked my foot around the front leg of his chair and kicked out. With a yelp, he fell flat on his back, his catapult backfiring and spraying mashed potatoes over his own face. I lifted the kid up by his shirt, so that his potato-covered face was only an inch from mine. Nicole was now forgotten; all eyes were on me.

"Mashed-potato catapult? Are you kidding?" I asked.

"What?"

"That's Ellie crap. Why don't you grow up?"

Before he could answer me, some clown shouted from the safety of the back. "Hey! Matt's in love with the pee-pee g—uuurk . . ." His little speech cut off in a strangled gurgle. The entire caf turned to see what had happened. Kevin stood there, the kid's throat in his hand. When the kid's face turned blue, Kev was nice enough to let him go. The rest of the caf resumed their lunch. I looked at Kevin and gave him a relieved little smile. He tried to return it, but his mouth couldn't remember how. It just twitched twice, quickly. Then he walked back to his table, to sit and brood over his untouched meal.

"You okay?" I asked Nicole. A look of defeat and a soft whimper were the only answers she gave me. She was wet and sticky from the milk, her eyes now more red than her hair. "C'mon," I said, and escorted her to the girl's bathroom. When she came out five minutes later, her hair still hung limp around her face, only now it was wet with water, not chocolate milk. A small improvement, but I'd take it.

I walked her over to an empty table and sat across from her. "Feel better?" I asked.

She nodded slightly, without looking me in the eye.

"You hungry?" I asked, as I put my brown-bagged lunch on the table.

She shook her head no.

"You sure? I have a chocolate chip cookie." I felt like I was talking to someone half her age.

She sat silently for a moment, as if she hadn't heard me. Just as I was about to ask her again, her head bobbed up and down slightly. I put my hand in the bag. As I was pulling it out, she flinched, as if she were expecting me to have a squirt gun. I showed her the cookie I had promised, put it on a napkin, and slid it across the table to her. Her fingers touched the edge of the napkin and slid it the rest of the way. She picked up the cookie gingerly, as if it were made of glass, took a tiny nibble, then put the cookie back down. I watched her for a long time, trying to figure out what to say, rejecting every thought before it hit my lips. She kept repeating the eating motion with the cookie. At that rate, she'd finish it just before spring break.

I pulled the half picture of Joey out of my pocket. Again, she flinched as my hand came up. She started to breathe again when she saw the photo. I slid it over to her. "You know this kid?" I asked, tapping the picture twice.

"Joey," she whispered, as if the name itself had power. She must have heard the stories, that it was Joey who took her out. She acted afraid, as if he was going to pop out of the picture and take her down again.

"This is a picture from a newspaper," I said, "an Ellie newspaper. Do you remember it?" She shook her head no. "Do you know who was in the other half of this photo?" She shook her head no again. She never took her eyes off the picture of Joey. Her whole body started to shake, as if the temperature in the cafeteria had dropped thirty degrees. Her eyes welled up with tears, but none of them fell.

"You okay?" I asked, but I wasn't sure I cared. I was frustrated. Nikki Fingers, once the most fearsome girl in school, was reduced to this: a terrified little girl, scared to death of a picture from a newspaper, unable to answer simple questions or even look me in the eyes. Suddenly, I grabbed her hand. She flinched and started to shrink away, as if I was going to drag her off and humiliate her further. A frightened moan came from the back of her throat.

"Listen to me," I hissed, "you're Nikki Fingers for Chrissakes! You could chew these kids up and spit them out, one at a time or all together. You don't belong in the Outs, and it's time to stop acting like you do."

For an impromptu speech, I didn't think it was half bad, until I let go of Nicole's hand. She snapped it back as if it were on a retractable cord, then stood up from the table quickly and awkwardly, as if she wasn't sure her legs would support her. She was still shaking as she walked away, drawing her arms in, trying to make herself as small as possible. She didn't look back.

"Nice speech, Matthew." Vinny walked up behind me and sat down in the seat Nicole had vacated.

"Yeah, it really worked wonders."

"She needs a little more than a speech, don't you think?"

"I was hoping I had a couple more years before I had to figure out what girls need."

He nodded. "You and me both."

"I just don't get it . . . How she can go from being Nikki to being . . . that." Nicole was wandering aimlessly around the lunchroom. Kids were throwing French fries at her; she didn't seem to notice.

"The school turned against her. No kid, even someone as fierce as Nikki, stands a chance against the *entire* school."

"I don't buy it. If anyone stands a chance, it's Nikki."

"This isn't Ellie, Matthew. You can't just hand out cupcakes and change the school's opinion of you."

"No, but you *can* use cat pee. Personally, I'd rather have the cupcake."

Vinny shrugged, closing the issue as far as he was concerned. He looked at the newspaper photo that I had put on the table earlier. "He looks so young," he said, referring to the Joey in the picture, the Joey from two years ago.

"Yeah, they grow up fast."

"He was a good soldier," Vinny said.

"I'm sure he's taking a lot of comfort in that right now."

"Look, Matthew, if I got taken out tomorrow, I couldn't expect my past to protect me from my future."

"You expecting to get hit tomorrow?"

"Hardly. But you're missing my point."

"Maybe I'm not missing it. Maybe I just don't think it applies to every situation."

"That has yet to be proven. Listen, you know as well as I do, once you're convicted by a jury of your peers, it's hard to get a new trial."

"And you, the mighty Vinny Biggs, can't do anything to help them out?"

"Matthew, I'm like a big ship in this ocean. Sure, I can pretty much go where I want, but I don't have power over the tides. Some things are too big for even me to control. Public opinion is one of them."

"Bull. If you wanted to get Nicole back in, you could."

"Nobody gets back in," he said, a trace of sadness in his voice.

"Even your favorite?"

"Especially my favorite. Now kids know that if the infamous Nikki Fingers can't escape the Outs, then nobody can. That's a powerful statement."

"I'm sure she'd be happy to hear that. 'Hey, Nicole, your life's in the crapper, but good news! Now you're a powerful statement!' "

"Matthew, I've got a whole operation to worry about, and I can't go out on a limb for one girl—" He paused for a moment. "No matter how I feel about her."

"Ahh, loyalty. Remind me again why I didn't join your 'operation.' Oh, wait . . . you just did."

Vinny's good humor disappeared. "Don't ever question my loyalty to my people, Matthew."

"Threat?"

"Warning."

"You can take your warnings, Vinny, and shove 'em up your—" A small commotion stopped me before I dug my own grave. Nicole had wandered back over, looking lost, but knowing exactly where she was going. Vinny's guards were trying to hold her back, but delicately, with respect for who she once was. That respect was making their job harder.

"Vinnnnyyyy!" she cried out, in an eerie voice that sounded like a hinge someone forgot to oil. "Vinnnyyyyy! Whyyy . . . Vinnnnyyyy . . ." She stumbled toward him. Vinny was wearing a cool and unaffected look, but underneath there was a subtle hint of fear. "Whhhyyyy???" she howled. "Whyyyyyy???? Vinnnyyyy!"

The last "Vinny" was a high-pitched shriek, like a bucket of ice water to the face. The entire cafeteria seemed to jump at the same time. Nicole's voice dissolved into sobs as she broke down, falling to her knees in front of Vinny. Vinny slumped his shoulders like a beaten man, all his talk about the "importance of his operation" evaporating. He nodded his head to the right, signaling to his guards to get her out of there; they obliged, dragging her off. Her sobs echoed through the now silent cafeteria.

"Great display of loyalty," I said to Vinny with disgust.

"Matthew," he said in a voice that tried to sound threatening, but was more tired and sad than fierce.

"Forget it. Save your energy. I'll finish this case and learn some manners." I picked up the photo and left.

I walked over to the pay phone in the hall, inserted the proper amount of change, and dialed Joey's number. If I could talk to him for five minutes, I'd be well on my way to solving this case. Still no answer. I hung up and retrieved my coins.

As I walked to my locker, I passed Kevin at his. "Hey," I said. "Nice choke hold at lunch today."

"You're welcome," he said to me, but his attention was on something over my shoulder. I turned to see what it was.

Nicole Finnegan, her hair a tangled mess, her eyes wide

and bloodshot, was shambling toward us. Kevin started looking for an escape route, but it was too late.

"Kevin!" she yelled, as if they were in the middle of a crowded stadium instead of a half-empty hallway.

"Hi, Nikki."

"Nikki?" She giggled. It was a jagged sound, like an out-of-tune piano. "Nikki's gone. Long gone. Only Nicole's left now."

"Okay," Kevin said. "Hi, Nicole."

"Better."

"Listen, I have to get to class . . ."

"What's wrong, Kevin?"

"Nothing, I just have to g—"

"Don't you like me anymore?"

He didn't answer her. The kids in the hall were laughing, but Nicole no longer heard them. She was tuned to a different frequency.

"You liked Nikki, didn't you? But you don't like Nicole . . . This is me now, Kevin." She spun around like a gear with a few teeth missing. "This is me!"

Kevin opened his mouth to speak, but nothing came out.

"I can be your girlfriend now, Kevin. Don't you want

me as a girlfriend?" She tried to fight back tears, but lost the battle. "Why don't you want me? I'm still me. I'm still me!" Her words and sobs started running together. Just then, Jenny broke through the crowd, grabbed her sister, and ushered her away. "I'm still me!" Nicole wailed, then disappeared out of sight. The crowd in the hall broke into applause.

Kevin rubbed his eyes and sighed.

"That went well," I said.

"I'm not in the mood, Matt."

"Way to stick by her, through thick and thin."

"Look, I saved your butt at lunch today, so cut me a little slack."

"Big deal. You saved me after I protected your girlfriend from taking another hit."

"She's not my girlfriend."

"Yeah. I got that."

"She wanted out, not me."

"And if she didn't, you'd be right there beside her now, slugging it out against the whole school," I said sarcastically.

"What do you want, Matt?"

I pulled out the picture of Joey from the Ellie newspaper. "You seen this before?"

"No," he said, but he dropped his gaze. He was lying.

"You want to help her? Then help *me!* You took out the wrong kid. Help me find the right kid."

"I've never seen it before!"

"You're lying. We both know it, so you might as well just stop."

He picked me up by the collar and slammed me into a row of lockers. I had pushed one button too many.

"Leave me alone," he said through gritted teeth.

"Carling!" Katie Kondo had come around the corner. She had missed most of the show, but managed to catch the last act. She wasn't a fan. "Drop him."

Kevin held me up for a moment longer, as if to say he'd let me go when he was ready.

"Drop him now, Kevin."

"Stay away from me, Matt. I mean it," Kevin hissed, then dropped me. I landed on my feet, my shirt disheveled. Kevin stomped his way down the hall and out of sight.

"You can thank me later," Katie said.

"Gee, how about I thank you now?" I said. "Thanks, Katie. Thanks for coming in at the exact moment that I was about to get some useful information."

"Watch your mouth, Stevens. You're lucky you're even allowed to operate."

"You need to learn a new line, Katie. That one's getting worn out."

She noticed the photo in my hand. "What's that?"

"Nothing. A memento of mine."

"Let me see it."

"Get lost."

"Hand it over, Matt. Now."

I sighed and passed it to her. She studied it for a second. "You withholding evidence?"

"No. It's a photo from an old newspaper. How's that evidence?"

"I don't know. You tell me."

"Nothing to tell."

"I'll find out on my own eventually."

"Great. Let me know how it turns out," I said. "I love a good mystery."

Her jaw tightened. She squinted her eyes and moved her face close to mine. To the casual observer, it would've looked like she was about to kiss me—or bite my nose off. "Enjoy this case, Matt. Really savor it," she said, "because it's your last."

We stared each other down, neither one of us willing to budge. Finally, the bell rang and broke the moment.

Katie folded up the photo, put it in her pocket, and walked off. Excellent. Not only did I not have any solid leads, but I also just lost the best piece of evidence I had. I congratulated myself on a job well done. At this rate, I wouldn't need Katie's help; I'd be washed up all on my own.

I got to my locker, cracked the lock, flicked the latch, opened the door, and jumped to the side. My luck was turning; no pee balloon flew out at me this time. Instead, a piece of purple paper fluttered to the floor. I picked it up cautiously, as if it might bite. It was a note from Jenny, on the same purple horse stationery that she had used before: "I had to take Nicole home, but call me tonight. Here's my number again, in case you lost it. Please be careful." It had her phone number at the bottom, and was signed with a heart, then her name. It was the first thing that made me smile all day, and another sign that maybe I should give

Jenny and me a shot. Why not? She was sweet, thoughtful, and damn good to look at. I decided to call her and see where it went. So what if she didn't give me the same feelings Liz did?

Liz. She still hadn't come to talk to me. In fact, I hadn't seen her around all day. Maybe she thought I blew her off last night by not answering the phone. I wanted to run to her locker and explain what happened, but I pushed the urge away. Liz and I would have to settle up later. Right now, I had to figure out what the hell I was doing about my job. There were only two classes to go before Thursday was in the books. Just one day left, and I was closer to going to a high school prom than I was to solving this case.

My best piece of evidence was now in the hands of the hall monitor chief. To be honest, even if I still had the Joey photo, it wasn't doing me much good. The other half was proving harder to find than a happy kid in a shoe store. While I was chasing it down, other pieces of evidence might have been slipping away.

At least I still had the note. I pulled it out and read it for the hundredth time: "Remember what we had. Do it or get out of the way. —B." All I knew was that "B" was a girl.

The case, as much as it made me a little nauseated to think about it, still hinged on Joey the Hyena's love life. Everyone I talked to so far had testified to Joey's ability with the ladies. It still wasn't easy for me to swallow, but who was I to argue? My mind kept going back to the line: "Remember what we had." Joey may have shopped around, but there must have been something memorable about his relationship with "B" to make her believe she had an "in" like that.

I figured I'd check with Jimmy Mac first. He made his living out of watching people. I caught up with him on my way to Algebra.

"No, I haven't found the photo yet. I would have called you if I did," he snapped before I had a chance to say anything. The frustration was obviously getting to him.

"All right. Don't pop a freckle."

"Sorry. . . . it's just . . ." He sighed. "This is a big story. And I *know* I have that picture somewhere. I'm just—"

"No, I know. Listen, forget the photo for a second. You said Joey went with a lot of girls, right?"

"Yeah."

"Do you remember any girl in particular? A girl you saw him with more than others?"

He gave himself a minute to review the tape running through his head.

"Nope. Wait—"

He cocked his head and squinted his eyes, as if an important piece of information was about to slide by, and he grabbed it just in time, right before it fell out of reach.

"I remember . . . The first time I noticed him, he was in this article we were doing on a group of girls."

"He was in a group of girls?"

"Yeah. Well, no. We were trying to get a picture of these girls, and he kept creeping into the background. We couldn't get one clean shot without him."

"What group?

"Ohhhh . . . What were they called? Some goofy name . . ." He snapped his fingers twice, as if that would help. "You should ask Jenny."

"Finnegan?"

"Yeah. She was in it."

The bell rang.

"Listen," Jimmy Mac said, backing away from me, "I can't afford to be late to another class."

"Yeah. Me, neither. Hey, do me a favor—" I started to ask.

"Dig up that article?"

"How'd you guess?"

"Superior intellect."

"You should use that superior intellect to get your crap organized."

"I'll try, Mom!" he yelled from down the hall.

I barely squeaked through my last classes. This case was taking up all of my available brain space, and Algebra and Social Studies weren't about to dislodge it.

I raced out of class as soon as the bell rang. I was desperate to talk to Jenny, if only to make this lead less dependent on Jimmy Mac and his paper chaos. I pulled out the note with her number on it, went to the pay phone in the hall, and called her. For the millionth time, I wished I could afford a cell phone.

The phone rang twice before Jenny picked up. "Hello?"

"Hey, Jenny. It's Matt."

"Hi, Matt." I could feel her smile over the line. "I didn't expect you to call so soon. Did you find something out?"

"Maybe. Were you in a group in Ellie?"

"A group?"

"Yeah. A bunch of girls. Gave yourselves a funny name . . ."

"The Fourth-Grade Parade?"

I laughed. I couldn't help it.

"What?" she asked, puzzled as to why a name like "the Fourth-Grade Parade" was funny.

"Who was in your group?" I asked.

"Me, Jean Polio, Rachel Farnsworth, a couple of girls whose families moved, Melanie, Liz . . ."

"Melanie and Liz?"

"Yeah. We had known each other for years, but it wasn't until fourth grade that we really started hanging out. We started doing those pageants. Remember those?"

"Vaguely. They used to troop us down to the cafeteria to watch."

"I think you older kids thought we were dorks, but we didn't care. We got to dress up, get out of class, dance in front of an audience . . . We had so much fun."

"Was Joey Renoni part of your group?"

"Nope. It was just us girls. He just liked to hang

out with us a lot. I think he like liked a couple of the girls, but we were all so young then, nobody even knew what that meant. We were just having fun."

"Which girls did he like like? Do you remember?"

"Not really. He went through so many."

"Yeah, I've heard. Any members of the Fourth-Grade Parade have a 'B' in their name?"

She thought about it for a second. "One. Betty Thomas. She was one of the girls who moved away."

"Figures."

"Why? Does this have something to do with my sister?"

"I'm not sure yet. Listen, I have to go. I'll call you later."

"Promise?"

"Absolutely," I said, but I wasn't sure if I meant it. We said our good-byes and hung up. I sprinted off to try to catch Jimmy Mac before he left school.

My luck, like the weather, had once again turned from good to bad. Usually Jimmy Mac stayed at school pretty late, setting up the layout for the next day's newspaper. That day, however, was the first time in weeks that he had to leave early. Dentist appointment. I went outside and unlocked my bike, feeling the first couple of raindrops hit my arm. I was going to have to hurry if I didn't want to get soaked.

Of course, the rain started to fall harder when I was halfway home. By the time I got there, I was more than a little damp. As I was unlocking the outside door to my office, I could hear the phone ringing inside. I hustled to get it before whoever it was hung up. On the seventh ring, I picked it up.

"Yeah."

A hushed voice greeted me on the other end. "Matt?" I couldn't tell who it was.

"Yeah?"

"It's Mac."

"Hey, I was looking for you. I thought you had a dentist appointment."

"I did. No cavities."

"Congratulations. Listen, I need that article on the Fourth-Grade Parade, plus anything you can dig up on Mel Kondo and Liz—"

"Matt," he interrupted, "you have to meet me at Sal's."

"What? Right now? It's pouring out."

"You're gonna want to see this."

I took a moment. "You found the picture," I said.

"I found the picture."

"Who's in it?"

"Not over the phone."

"Why not?"

"You have to trust me," he said. Then I heard his mom

yelling in the background. Mac yelled back. "I'll be off in a sec, Ma!"

"Fine," I said. "I'll meet you at Sal's."

"See ya there," he said, and hung up. I looked around my office, taking a minute to soak in the warmth. Sal's wasn't far from me, but it was getting bad out. It didn't matter. I'd ride my bike through a tornado to get a lead in this case. I just hoped it wouldn't come to that.

I grabbed my bike and was about to head out when the phone upstairs started ringing. I dropped my bike and ran upstairs. I knew who it was before I picked up the phone.

"Hi, Mom."

"Matt. How'd you know it was me?"

"Psychic. Don't worry, I'm home."

"So you're safe and sound?"

"Yup. Inside, warm and cozy."

"Good. I hated thinking you might be out in this downpour."

"Nope. Your son's smart enough to stay out of the rain," I said, and almost kept a straight face. "Listen, I'm going to go do my homework, then maybe take a nap. Someone kept me out late last night."

"You call nine thirty late?"

"For a young, innocent lad such as myself, nine thirty is—"

"Young, innocent lad? Puh-leeze. I don't remember ordering the baloney special."

"Forget it. You know, sometimes I don't even know why I talk to you."

"Because I'm your gorgeous mother and you love me."

"And you feed me."

"And I feed you. Although, I'm really starting to reconsider that." In the background, I heard Mr. Carling bark at my mom to get off the phone. "I have to go."

"Right. Give Mr. C a big kiss for me," I said.

"Don't even joke about that."

"Who's joking?"

"Ugh . . . Love ya."

"You, too. Bye." She hung up quickly, leaving me to wonder if she was getting yelled at. I felt helpless and a little guilty for lying to her, but I pushed those feelings away. I had no time for self-pity. I grabbed the bottle of chewable vitamins on the counter, shook a couple out, and popped them in my mouth. The chalky, artificial taste of grape coated my mouth. If I was going to dodge a cold, I needed all the help I could get.

It wasn't as bad outside as I thought it was going to be; it was worse. The chill in the air, combined with the steady rain, made my legs feel like rusted iron. Every pump of my legs was an effort. The windbreaker I wore was immediately outmatched. I should have just worn a bathing suit and snorkel.

As I rode, I thought of Liz. I still hadn't heard from her, and I wasn't sure what to say if and when we finally did talk. I liked her a lot, but I couldn't overlook her blindness when it came to her brother. She loved Kevin, which was understandable, but she'd never find fault with his actions, which wasn't. Joey was a rat and deserved exactly what Kevin gave him, but that wasn't the point. It wasn't up to Kevin to give it to him.

I thought about how much easier my life would be if those things didn't bother me. I thought of all the other kids in my class who didn't give a damn who did what to whom, as long as it didn't directly affect them. I thought about all the friendships I killed because of my need for the truth. I thought of Kevin and Liz.

Then I thought about the kid behind this whole

Nikki mess: her smug smile as she sat contented in the belief that she had gotten away with it, that there was nobody in school smart or determined enough to bring her down. I thought of her watching the time run out on my investigation, and I could almost hear her laughing at me. And all I wanted to do, with every fiber of my being, was drag her out into the open and let her know, in no uncertain terms, that she chose the wrong kid to screw with. I pedaled harder.

Sal's was packed. It was standing room only, and there was barely room for that. Sal had the heaters going, but instead of being cozy, it was humid and uncomfortable, like a greenhouse in July. I started to break into a sweat, which mingled strangely with the rainwater. I expected to see steam rising off my clothes.

Jimmy Mac was sitting at a table alone, one seat saved for me. "Hey, Matt. I didn't expect it to be this busy. Lot of kids drowning their sorrows."

"Yeah, must've been a lot of pop quizzes today. You got the photo?"

"Yeah," he said, but in a way that made my stomach drop. He looked like he had news, all of it bad, like a paperboy during the Great Depression. "I found it in a box in my closet."

"Let's see it," I said.

Just then, Sal came over to take our order. "Hey, guys. Busier than I expected."

"Yeah," Mac said, frowning. "I'll just have a root beer."

"Same," I said. Sal went off to get them. I turned to Mac. "Let's see it."

"It could be a mistake."

"Just put it on the table, Mac. We'll make sense of it after I look."

He nodded the way you do when you have to do something you don't want to do. He put his hand in the inside pocket of his jacket and pulled out a plastic sandwich bag. The photo was inside, so the rain wouldn't ruin it. He took it out and put it on the table.

I looked at it. It wasn't a newspaper clipping; it was the actual photo, in color. Joey was still smiling at the camera, with the lovesick grin that I remembered so well. Sitting next to him, smiling a smile that I had seen hundreds of times, was Liz Carling. There was a caption, handwritten on another piece of paper and taped to the bottom of the photo; it said: "Joey Renoni and Elizabeth Carling, 'just friends.'"

The cramp I felt in my stomach was the first indication that what I was seeing was real. My brain didn't want to believe it, but my stomach already knew it was true. All my energy for this case seeped out of me. "Did kids used to call her Beth in Ellie?" I asked Mac.

"How would I know?"

"You run a newspaper. It's your job to know."

He sighed and looked away from me.

"Did kids in Ellie call her Beth?" I asked again.

"Yeah," he answered quietly, as if he hated to admit it.

I pulled the note that Joey had given me, right before he had been rubbed out. It still said, "Remember what we had. Do it or get out of the way," and it was still signed, "B."

I sighed and rested my head in my hands. Sal came over with our drinks.

"Here ya go." He put them down, and looked at us. "You guys okay? You look like your dog died."

"We're fine," Mac answered.

"Okay," Sal said, clearly thankful that we weren't going to spill our guts to him. He was too busy to sit and listen.

After he hurried off, Mac and I sat in silence for a few minutes. Finally, Mac looked at me. "What are you going to do?" he asked.

"I'm going to ask her out for ice cream."

"Seriously?"

"No. I'm going to take her in."

"Yeah, but—" He paused.

"But what?"

"But . . . you like her, right?"

I was startled and couldn't hide it. It's always a shock to learn that you're transparent. "Maybe. I like a lot of people," I said, trying to cover.

"Matt, it's not like I'm going to do a story on it."

"If you already know, why are you asking me?"

Mac shot me an amused look. "I'm a reporter. I always check my facts."

"All right, fine. I like her, but just a little, and less by the second."

"So what are you going to do?"

"Check it out. What else can I do?"

"Does she have a motive?"

"Yeah. Nikki wasn't on Liz's list of favorites."

"How come?"

"Kevin had a crush on Nikki."

"Who didn't?"

"And Nikki broke his heart."

"She broke a lot of hearts."

"Yeah, but Kevin's is the only one Liz cares about."

"Hmm," Jimmy said, nodding his head. "You really think Liz is capable of taking someone out?"

I thought back to the Peter Kuhn case: the kid with the perfect life who threw it all away for a bunch of Pixy Stix. "Anybody's capable of anything," I said.

"Yeah, but she's so . . ."

"Small? Cute? Sounds a lot like Nikki when she first got started."

"Yeah," he paused, letting the noise from the room fill the gap. "I'm sorry, Matt."

"Yeah. Me, too. It sucks when the girl you like is a cold-blooded assassin." I couldn't help but laugh. "I doubt that'll be on a greeting card anytime soon."

We both laughed a little harder than the joke deserved. I downed the rest of my root beer in three big gulps. I needed it.

"You okay?" Jimmy asked.

"Sure."

"You don't look it."

"Listen, Mac, I've got to wrap up this case by tomorrow, and this is the first break I've gotten. I've fallen hard for Liz, no doubt. But if she did it, I'm bringing her down, and I've got enough dough coming my way to make sure I've at least got a soft landing."

"You sure that's not the root beer talking?"

"No."

"Well, at least you're honest."

I stood up and threw a couple of bucks on the table. "I'll see you tomorrow Mac, let you know how it all turns out."

"Where you going?"

"Santini's."

19

Santini's was in a two-story Colonial built sometime in the mid-1800s. The clapboard shingles had so many coats of white paint that it would take you a couple of hours to drill through it to get to the wood. The black decorative shutters were put up to give it that authentic, old-timey New England look, although I doubted they had molded plastic in the 1800s. It had been converted into a restaurant around 1967, when Mr. Santini took a gamble that people would pay to feel like they were having dinner at a friend's house. He was right.

Thursday was Kevin and Liz's night to help their dad

out at the restaurant, so I knew she'd be there. It was a bad decision to go there, but I didn't care. I had to talk to her, and it had to be right now.

Janine, the hostess, met me at the door. I could hear the hum of the dinner rush in the next room. "Hi, Matt! Little wet out there, huh?"

"Where's Liz?" I asked. It was almost a yell.

"Oh, uhhh, I think she's in the kitchen. Do you want me to get your mom?"

Before I could answer, Kevin came out, wearing a navy blue suit, with a white shirt and a red tie. "What do you want?" he asked.

"Nice suit. Where's Liz?"

"Get out of here, Matt."

"No. I need to talk to Liz. Bring her out, or these people are going to get dinner and a show."

"Not gonna happen."

"Around you or through you, Kev. What's it going to be?"

"Oh, right, Matt. What are you gonna—" I tackled him. We went tumbling through the open doorway into the bar area. On our way, we hit the hostess stand with a thump, pushing it back with a violent squeak. Menus fell to the floor. Janine, who had been watching our exchange like it was a tennis match on fast forward, let out a yelp. Kevin was startled for a moment, giving me an advantage. I sat on his chest, my knees on his biceps, and pinned him to the floor. Water from my hair dripped into his face.

"I can't get Liz if you're sitting on me," he said.

"You weren't going to get her anyway."

"True."

"Stop it!" Janine yelled, pulling me off of Kevin. I struggled against her, but it was no use. Employees rushed over to see what the ruckus was all about.

"Matt?" I heard my mom ask from the back of the crowd.

I looked around. The once-loud dining room was now in shocked silence. Every eye in the place, from diner to employee, was on me. I started to feel a little self-conscious. I'd been right: It hadn't been such a great idea to come to Santini's.

"Matt, what are you doing here?" my mom asked.

Before I could answer her, Janine spoke for me. "He came in and tackled Kevin. For no reason!"

I had a reason, but not one I was willing to share with this audience. I stood there silently, wishing I could slip through the floorboards and disappear.

"Matt?" My mom waited for an explanation.

Mr. Carling stormed over like a cop at a street fight, saving me from having to make up an excuse. He was tall and used to be solid, but what was once in his chest was now in his stomach. He wore a dark suit that didn't hurt him, but didn't do him any favors, either, and his hair was dark and slicked back smooth against his skull. "Sorry for the interruption, folks," he said, addressing the dining room. "Please, go back to your meals." His voice was lighter than what you'd expect to come out of that body.

The audience paused a moment to consider how invested they were in seeing the outcome. Then the sounds of conversations and silverware clinks started up again, but a little more timid than before. They were keeping one eye on us, in case we did something interesting again, like throw a chair through a window.

With the crisis averted, Mr. Carling turned his attention to us. "What is going on here?" he said in a loud whisper through clenched teeth so white, I could practically see my reflection in them.

"Matt came in here and tackled Kevin!" Janine honked. "Then they started fighting."

"Is this true?" He tried to sound like a principal, but his voice lacked the authority. It didn't matter, though. I may not have had to answer to him, but my mom did. I looked at my shoes; they were the only things in the room that weren't judging me. I begrudgingly gave him a nod.

"Okay. Show's over. Get back to your tables," he said quietly to the crowd of employees. They dispersed slowly, as if they knew that the best was yet to come. Mr. Carling turned to my mom and put a finger in her face. "This is absolutely unacceptable!"

It was starting to sink in just how badly I had screwed this up. Not only had I let this case get to me, I had allowed it to bleed into my personal life. And now my mom was going to have to bear the brunt of it. It was unfair, but that was no excuse. Lots of things were unfair.

"Get your finger out of my face." The voice sounded like my mom's, but the tone was all wrong. Her voice had never sounded that flinty before.

"What did you say?" Mr. Carling's mouth hung open like a trapdoor.

"You heard me. Drop it or I bite it off."

"Don't you dare talk to me like that!"

"Or what? You'll fire me? Well, go ahead, Albert. Fire me."

Kevin and I stood watching, our mouths open as wide

as Mr. Carling's. A couple of tables stopped eating and started watching again.

"It's just three little words, Albert," my mom continued. "You've wanted to say them for so long. Here's your opportunity. Go ahead. Say them."

Mr. Carling looked as confused as he did angry. It was as if he had a million things that he wanted to say to my mom but they got jammed before he could get them out. He opened his mouth, then closed it quickly. Open. Close. Open. Close. You could see him rejecting ideas, one by one. Finally, he settled on, "Clean this up. Get back to work," and stormed off in the direction of the kitchen. "Kevin! Get over here!"

"We'll finish this tomorrow," Kevin said as he rushed off. He wanted it to sound tough, but it didn't. It's hard to be tough and confused at the same time.

I looked at my mom. I had so many questions, I didn't know which to ask first. "Mom?" was all I could muster.

"Go home, Matt," she said without looking at me. She bent over to pick up the fallen menus. "We'll talk about this later. Right now I have to get back to work."

"But Mom—"

"Matt!" she barked, startling me. "Get your butt back

home, now. You have questions? Well, so do I. But now's not the time, got it?"

I nodded, but kept my mouth shut. I had fulfilled my daily quota of stupidity.

"Good. Home." She pointed toward the door, in case I didn't know the way. I was so out of sorts that it actually helped.

As I turned to leave, I saw the kitchen door was open a crack. It was Liz. Her face looked tense. I wasn't going to get to her tonight, but there was no way she could hide from me at school tomorrow, and it looked like she knew it.

I went straight to my office when I got home. Before I did anything else, I pulled the sandwich bag of evidence out of my back pocket, just to make sure it was still intact. I looked at the photo; Joey and Liz smiled up at me from the past—young and innocent, without a care in the world. If they only knew then what they know now, their expressions would be drastically different.

My mom got home at 2:30 in the morning, late for a Thursday night shift. I assumed it was because she and Mr. Carling had a couple of things they needed to work out. She looked drained. I was wide awake.

"What the hell is going on?" she asked, diving right in.

"Nothing. Kev and I had a disagreement."

"In the middle of a Thursday rush?"

"It's a long story."

"Then you'd better start telling it."

"It's kind of . . . complex. Like what happened tonight between you and Mr. Carling. What was that?" I caught her off-guard. She hadn't expected me to go on the offensive so soon, and to be honest, neither had I.

"That's none of your business," she said, but she was rattled. "You're not in any position to ask questions."

"Why, because I'm a kid, or because of what happened tonight?"

"What do you think?"

"Personally, both."

"Oh yeah? You think if you were an adult, it would have been okay to barge into where I work and start fighting with my boss's son?"

"Maybe not, but if I were an adult, you might think I had a valid reason."

"And what reason is that?"

"I'll tell you if you tell me what happened between you and Mr. Carling."

"No, Matt. No bargains. We're not playing that game. I'm the mother in this relationship. Now tell me what the hell is going on!"

"Kevin and I had a fight."

"Why?"

"Sorry. I can't tell you. I guess you'll just have to punish me."

"Fine. You're punished," she said, but her heart wasn't in it. Law and order was never her strong suit.

"What happened between you and Mr. Carling?"

"Matt—"

"What?" I said, louder than I expected. "Tell me I'm too young. Tell me I wouldn't understand. Go ahead. Try."

She sighed and sat down at the edge of my bed. "You're not going to drop this until I tell you, are you?"

"Are you going to drop your questions about my fight with Kevin?"

"No."

"Well, there you go."

She paused. "Looks like we have some stuff we need to square up with each other."

"Yeah, looks like it."

We sat and looked at each other for a couple of minutes, neither one of us sure of where to start. Finally, my mom yawned.

"Not now," she said, "I'm too tired." She yawned again, as if to prove it.

"In the morning then."

"In the morning. And don't spend all night thinking of a cover story. I want the truth."

"Back atcha."

She smiled and raised one eyebrow. "I always knew you were going to be a handful."

"Funny," I said, "I was just thinking the same thing about you."

"Go to sleep." She turned and ambled off to bed.

I had no idea what I was going to tell her in the morning. I was so tired that it might have to be the truth. I wondered if she could handle knowing what was really going on at the Frank. I doubted it. My mom was pretty cool, but she had her limits. And if she blew the lid off of Vinny's whole operation, the only question would be which one of his assassins would put me in the Outs first.

I snapped awake the next morning, going from restless sleep to fully alert in less than a second. The queasy feeling I had in my stomach the night before was still there to greet me. I climbed out of bed and listened for my mom. Nothing. Either she wasn't awake yet or she had already left. I walked tentatively down the hall toward the kitchen. She was seated at the table, calmly drinking her coffee. She looked at me skulking down the hallway and smiled. I felt a little foolish.

"Good morning," she said. "Take a load off. You want something for breakfast?"

"I'll just have some cereal," I said, and went to the cabinet to get it. I poured myself a bowl before I realized I hadn't even had my orange juice yet. I pulled the OJ from the fridge and almost poured it over my cereal.

"Whoa," my mom said, "I'm not sure you want to do that."

I smiled sheepishly and grabbed a glass from the cabinet. "All right. I'll do it the normal way," I said sarcastically. "But I really think I was on to something."

"Crunchy orange juice?"

"Tangy cereal."

"Ohhhh."

I sat down and started eating my cereal. In the quiet of the kitchen, it sounded like I was chewing on gravel. My mom was looking at the morning paper, but kept glancing up at me every ten seconds. I had a feeling that if I asked her what story she was reading, she'd have no idea.

She put the paper down and cut to the chase. "Was the fight with Kevin over money?"

"No."

"Was it over drugs, or something illegal?"

"No. It wasn't about money, or drugs, or anything

illegal," I said, and left it at that. I was sure the next question was going to be what the fight was about.

It wasn't. She threw me a curveball instead. "Okay. I guess we have to make a deal then. You keep your secret, and I'll keep mine."

I looked at her with confusion and suspicion. Of all the things I was prepared for that morning, the deal she presented wasn't even on the list.

"You look surprised," she said.

"I am. I guess I expected you to bully me into submission. "

"How?

"With a mom's greatest weapons: guilt and punishment."

She shrugged. "I suppose I could get you to tell me your secret if I wanted to, but how is that good for either of us?"

"Well, it'd be good for you. You'd win."

"This isn't a contest, Matt. My mom was like that, and I—" She stopped, reconsidering what she was about to say. "I guess I see a lot of mothers act like that to their kids," she said, backpedaling. "Their kids end up hating them, and I guess I can't say I blame them. I'm not out to win every argument with you, Matt, because I'll lose you as a result." She paused. "I know this isn't the way most other mothers think, but then again, I don't like most other mothers."

I thought of Joey Renoni's mom: the way she yanked Joey around like an inexpensive handbag, not seeming to care that her screaming fits would do him more harm than good. I thought of Liz and Kevin's mom, and how she only acknowledged their existence when she needed to work out some of her frustrations. I thought of all the moms I've met since I started in this business. I could count on three fingers the kids who could go to their moms when they were really in a jam. Most kids felt like when they were home, they were behind enemy lines. So what my mom was saying made sense, but I wasn't sure I trusted it just yet. "What's your angle?" I asked.

"No angle. That's the deal." She took a deep breath and let it out slowly. "There are things in my life, Matt, that I'm not ready to talk about. Not with anybody, even you."

I thought about my mom's family, and her past, of which I knew so little. I thought about my dad, and the clue the police had found in his abandoned car; the clue that my mom denied knowing anything about, but had caused such a marked change in her behavior.

"It stings a little," she said. "I know. But I have a feeling you're in the same boat."

"No, Mom, I just—"

"It's okay," she said, putting her hand out to stop me. "It's natural. It's part of growing up. Even the people you love, the people you're closest to, can't share everything with you. Some things you just have to keep to yourself.

"Look," she continued, "I can't fix all your problems for you, and you can't expect me to. That wouldn't be doing either one of us any good." She broke into a smile. "Plus, I have a feeling you can navigate your problems just fine without me."

I smiled back at her. "I do all right."

"So that's the deal. Take it or leave it."

Before I could take it, she put her hand up. "Wait. Sorry. There is one condition."

"Yeah?"

"If you find yourself in a jam that even *you* can't handle, come to me. We'll try to work it out together. Deal?"

"Only if you promise to do the same."

She gave a little laugh.

"You'd be surprised at what I'm capable of," I said.

"You're wrong. I don't think I'd be surprised at all. Deal." She held out her hand to shake. I got up from the table, walked over and grabbed it. We shook twice, then she pulled me in for a kiss. "Love you."

"You too, Mom."

She looked at the clock. "Seven fifteen. Go get ready for school."

"Yup." I headed toward the bathroom to take a shower. "I'll see you tonight."

"Okay. Good luck at school today," she said.

"When you're good, you don't need luck."

"Oh, well then definitely good luck."

"Ouch. Get out of here. Go mother someone else."

When I got out of the shower, she was gone. I got dressed, went downstairs to grab the evidence I still had, then headed off to school. I took my time walking. I was dreading the face-off with Liz that was waiting for me, but I tried not to think about it. It was the kind of fall morning that tourists came to New England for: crisp, cool, and sunny, and I just wanted to enjoy it. The sunlight filtered through the multicolored leaves, giving the outside a warm, syrupy quality, like an old photograph that was slightly out of focus. Six Ellie kids ran past me, amped up with the kind of energy that only comes this time of year, with all the best holidays fast approaching. All six of them turned and gave me a raspberry. I gave one back. They ran off giggling. I smiled and made a silent wish for them: *May their lives always be as simple as they are now.* It was a foolish hope, because it just wasn't possible. When you got older, things got more complicated; that was the way the world worked. Of all the lessons I'd learned at the Frank, it was the only one I was certain of.

When I got to school, I headed straight for Liz's locker. It was Friday, so kids were bouncing around the hall like Super Balls shot from a rocket launcher. Liz had just closed her locker and turned to go to class when she saw me and stopped dead in her tracks. We faced off against each other like a couple of reluctant gunslingers. Kids walked around and through our path, oblivious to what was going down. I envied them. I walked toward her, closing the gap.

"Morning, Matt."

"Liz."

"Heard you came to the restaurant last night."

"Yeah. I wanted to see the specials."

"What happened with Kevin?"

"I was upset you were out of shrimp." I pulled out the picture of her and Joey. "Recognize this?"

"Of course."

"Want to tell me about it?"

"Not much to tell. We went to a spring dance together. Someone snapped a picture. We both moved on with our lives."

"Why him?"

"He asked me. Nobody else did," she said accusingly.

"You went by the name 'Beth' then, right?"

"I still go by Beth when someone calls me that. It's part of my name."

"What about this?" I asked, pulling out the note signed by "B." "Recognize it?"

"No."

"Here. Maybe you're not looking close enough." I handed it to her.

"'Do it or get out of the way. —B,'" she read. "You think I'm 'B' because I sometimes go by the name Beth and I'm in an old photo with Joey?"

"These two were in an envelope together. Joey had them on him right before your brother took care of him." She winced, but I pressed on. "You never liked Nikki after what she did to Kevin."

"You're wrong about that. I didn't like her before then."

"This is serious, Liz."

"I know. And I'm being serious, Matt," she said in a mocking tone. "By all means, continue your accusation."

"Did you do it?" I asked.

"Did I do what?"

"You know what."

"I do, but I want you to say it."

I ran my hand over my mouth.

"It's hard for you," she said. "Good. It should be."

"Did you take Nikki out?"

"No."

"I don't believe you," I said.

"I know, but I wish you did."

"Come on, Liz, don't make this harder than it has to be."

"Oh, I'm not going to make it hard. I'm going to make it really easy." Her tone of voice was sad, but her eyes were furious. "If that's the best you've got for evidence, then get lost. Katie'll never go for it, no matter how much she hates my brother and me."

"I could convince her of the truth."

"Is that really what you think of me, Matt? You think I could take someone out in cold blood like that?"

"I believe you can do anything you set your mind to."

She slapped me hard across the face. "Hey, what do you know? You were right."

I rubbed my jaw. Unlike Jenny, Liz packed a wallop. One of my loose molars popped out of its socket.

"Until you apologize or get more evidence, don't talk to me. Got it?" She stormed off without waiting for an answer.

I was still rubbing my jaw when Jimmy Mac came up behind me. "Man, that looked like it hurt."

"You have no idea," I said, then spit out the tooth. "Looks like I'll be getting a visit from the tooth fairy."

"Yeah. Well, before I forget, here." Jimmy handed me a bunch of newspaper clippings.

"What are these?"

"Yesterday, you asked me for anything I had on Melanie Kondo. I dug these up."

The top article was from the Ellie paper a few years ago, introducing the newest batch of hall monitors for the year. Melanie was mentioned.

"What grade was she in when she joined the monitors?" I asked.

"Third. Youngest ever selected."

"She was that good?"

"Just the opposite. She was running with the wrong crowd, and Katie tried to straighten her out."

I nodded. "It's a hard life, especially when you're young. You've really got to love the sash."

"I think it's fair to say that Mel doesn't," Mac said. I nodded in agreement.

I flipped through the other articles in the pile. Melanie was mentioned as the hall monitor on the scene for some minor incidents, most involving crackdowns on runners in the halls. The last one was the one I wanted. It was a pretty big story about the Fourth-Grade Parade.

"You found it?" I said.

"Don't sound so surprised," Mac answered.

It was a run-of-the-mill Ellie puff piece, talking about who the girls were, where they got their ideas, which songs they'd performed. At the time of the article, the most recent song they'd done was "You Are My Sunshine." A memory I forgot I had popped into my head. I remembered trooping into the cafeteria/auditorium/gym in the middle of the day, glad for any break in the daily routine. I remembered how the room had a weird, musty smell, like old clothes and paste. I remembered how cold and uncomfortable those metal folding chairs were. They had to be. The heat was cranked up to 85 degrees. If the chairs had been comfortable, I'd still be asleep there.

I remembered the first few notes of "You Are My Sunshine" blaring out over the P.A. system. The acoustics of the room were so bad that it took a minute before you knew what the song was, even though the title was written on signs all over the place. When the song started, Big Bobby Wetner came out on stage dressed as the sun. The audience almost erupted into laughter. Almost. Big Bobby was in fifth grade at the time, and he was almost twice the size of everybody else. The look on his face dared anyone in the audience to laugh at him. Nobody took him up on it. The rumor was that someone had caught Bobby with a cheat sheet in Math, and they gave him a choice: be the sun in the pageant or face the consequences. It had to be a kid who caught him. No teacher would ever give him a deal like that. Still, watching him on stage, his legs bulging in tights like bright yellow sausages, I wondered if he had made the right decision.

Soon the stage was full of little girls dressed as various things in nature: flowers, birds, insects. I recognized a few of the girls: Jenny was a dragonfly, Liz was a butterfly, Mel was a— I stopped reminiscing for a second and hit the rewind button on my memory. I remembered watching Melanie dance and thinking how much she looked like a smaller, more relaxed version of her sister. She was dancing around the stage with a look of complete joy. Her face was just barely poking out of a costume that was a little too big for her . . . a costume that I had completely forgotten about until this very moment. A quick scan of the news story confirmed it.

"You okay, Matt?"

"Here," I said, handing Jimmy the article. "Read the fourth paragraph out loud."

"'Playing the role of the sun was fifth grader Bobby Wetner,'" Jimmy read. "I remember that! He looked ridicul—"

"Keep reading."

"Right. 'Fourth grader Elizabeth Carling played the

butterfly, the part of the bumblebee was played by'—" He stopped short with a gasp. A small smile creased his face. "Bee," he said.

"Bee," I repeated as confirmation. I read the note aloud: "'Do it or get out of the way. —B.'" It wasn't an initial from a name, it was a shorthand version of a nickname. I looked at the photo of Joey and Liz at the Spring Fling. This time, it looked different to me. Joey looked like he might be more interested in the photographer than in the girl he was sitting with. "Who took this picture?" I asked.

"I don't remember," Jimmy said, "But the initials of whoever did are written in the back right corner."

He was right. There they were, written in pencil so faint, you'd have to be looking for them to find them. I smiled again. I showed Jimmy. They matched the initials of the girl who played the bumblebee, the girl who it appeared had set Joey up, and taken Nikki out.

"You ready for your story?" I asked Mac.

"Does a nerd hate gym class?" he replied.

22

The bell had rung. The hallway had emptied out except for one girl in an ill-fitting orange sash, standing at her locker, talking to her sister. Actually, her sister was talking to her, but she didn't seem to be listening. She kept stealing anxious glances down the hallway, almost as if she was looking for someone specific. When she saw me coming, there was a strange expression on her face, a weird mixture of relief and hatred. I was who she was looking for. She had been waiting for me.

"Hi, Bee," I said to her.

Melanie Kondo sneered back at me. "Don't talk to me."

"Too late, Bee."

Katie looked at me, a little slow on the uptake. "What the hell's going on, Stevens?"

"Why don't you ask your sister?"

"Because I'm asking you."

"Fine. I'll tell it. Melanie is the little 'B' that put the sting on Nikki Fingers."

"This better be a joke, Stevens," Katie said.

"You see me laughing?"

Katie's face turned bright red, like an overripe tomato.

"No, but in a second, I'm going to see you crying." She advanced on me, ready to make good on her promise.

"Better watch it. The press is here," I said, pointing to Jimmy Mac. "Police brutality stories sell lots of papers, right, Mac?" Mac looked a little overwhelmed, as if he wasn't sure if he should eat his pencil or use it to write something down.

Katie changed tactics. "Melanie, what's he talking about?"

I had the advantage. I had to press it. "It was Joey Renoni's pet name for you, wasn't it? He called you 'Bee' after you played one in 'You Are My Sunshine' back in fourth. He had a crush on you, but you just wanted to be friends. You were saving yourself for someone else: Kevin."

Melanie didn't say a word. A tear rolled silently down her cheek.

"Joey asked you to the fifth-grade Spring Fling, but you said no, hoping that Kevin would. Kevin never did, so you picked up a job snapping pics for the newspaper." I pulled out the photo from my bag of evidence. "It was you who took this shot of Joey and Liz. Your initials are on the back. M.K." I turned the photo and showed her. She didn't look, but Katie did.

"You gave this photo to Joey, with this note that said, 'Do it or get out of the way. —B,' when you asked him to take out Nikki for you."

"That's enough, Matt," Katie said, but her voice lacked any real strength. I ignored her.

"You hoped that Joey still had a soft spot in his heart for you. He did. Unfortunately for you, he didn't have a soft spot in his head. He turned you down. He always talked about taking Nikki out, but he always knew that if he did, there'd be a price to pay. It was too steep a price just to fulfill an Ellie crush. You had to go with Plan B."

Melanie's tears flowed freely. I felt bad for her, but I didn't stop.

"You had spent enough time with Joey to get his laugh down pat. You knew if you just covered your face, you could pass for him in a crowded hallway, especially with everyone distracted by Nikki. All you had to do was throw out the laugh and hope kids bit. They did."

Katie looked at her sister as if she wasn't sure she recognized her. "Mel . . . Tell him it's not true." Melanie looked at her sister with tear-filled eyes, her breath going in and out in a sharp staccato rhythm.

"It is true," I said. "When I punched Kevin two days ago, you looked like you wanted to boil me in the lunch lady's chili. What would you do to someone who really hurt Kevin, someone like Nikki, who also happened to be your main competition? Easy. You bought her a one-way ticket to the Outs. And it didn't matter. Not one bit. Kevin still doesn't know you're alive."

"You're wrong! He loves me! He said we'd be together!" Melanie said, then immediately clapped her hand over her mouth. She had said more than she wanted to, and it was too late for a do-over.

"Did Kevin put you up to it?" Katie asked.

Melanie didn't answer. She just stood there with her

eyes wide and her mouth covered.

"Did Kevin put you up to it?" Katie asked again. "Answer me!"

"*No!* It was *my* idea! He had nothing to do with it!" Melanie yelled back, putting herself between her locker and Katie.

Katie pushed her out of the way. Melanie fell to the ground, butt first. She made a desperate attempt to scramble to her feet, to try to stop Katie from opening her locker. It was too late. The Super Soaker that fell out was almost as big as Melanie. It was a wonder she was able to lift it, let alone fire it. It had once been bright yellow, but had been painted a subtle green to make it easier to hide. Katie stared at it, as if it were an exotic new species of animal, one that she had read about in stories but never thought existed. Melanie tried to get to her feet, ignoring the squirter. She was trying to get to something else, something that was still in her locker. Katie got there first.

There, on the top shelf, was a stack of notes. Katie pulled them down and looked at them. Melanie screamed and clawed, trying to get them out of her sister's hands. What she lacked in aim, she made up for in intensity. Some of the shots connected below the belt. Mac and I both cringed, but Katie didn't even seem to notice, another reminder of the difference between boys and girls.

Melanie stopped attacking and started pleading. "Please, Katie. Don't." I felt really bad for her. She was looking for mercy from Katie, the hardest case in middle school, which was kind of like looking for tofu at a barbecue joint. Katie was her sister, her own blood, and it didn't matter one bit.

"He made you to do it," Katie said.

"No!" Melanie shouted. "I hated her! I wanted to do it!" She started to sob again.

Katie handed me the letters. "What do they say, Stevens?" she asked in a wooden voice.

The top letter was in Kevin's handwriting, but the words sounded nothing like him. It was a proclamation of love, written in language so flowery, my allergies almost acted up. At the bottom of the page was his signature, written in his neat, compact script. I flipped through the rest of the letters, skimming for content. Melanie tried to claw her way toward them, screaming and sobbing. Katie held her back.

A few phrases jumped out at me. "Do it and we can be together" was one of them. "Nikki's the only thing standing in our way" was another. I started to see the outline of the plan as it had happened: the suggestion to go to Joey to see if he would do the job, the idea for the backup plan in case he wouldn't, even a brief description of how to imitate his laugh; it was all there, signed by Kevin.

"Is that his handwriting?" Katie asked.

"How would I know? What do you think, we pass love notes to each other in class?" I said.

"Is that his handwriting?"

"Katie, I don't know—"

"You know, Matt! I know you know! So just cut the crap and tell me!"

Yeah, I knew, but something was holding me back from ratting him out. Maybe it was the friendship Kevin and I once had. Maybe it was a nagging feeling that something wasn't right. Whatever it was, Katie wasn't going to give me time to think about it. She grabbed the front of my shirt and slammed me into the lockers.

"Look . . . bad . . . in the paper," I sputtered, pointing to Mac. That ploy had worked earlier, but Katie didn't care about her image in the paper anymore. She didn't care about losing her post as hall monitor chief. The only thing she cared about was nailing Kevin Carling.

"Is. That. His. Handwriting?"

"Did. You. Have. Bologna. For. Lunch?" She would've

strangled me right there if Liz and Jenny hadn't walked up at that moment.

"Looks like you're making lots of friends today, Matt," Liz said.

"Just call me Mr. Popular."

Katie dropped my shirt and grabbed the notes from me in one swift motion. She shoved the notes into Liz's hands. "Is that your brother's handwriting?"

"What's going on?"

"Answer the question!"

Liz glanced at what she was holding. "Yeah, I think so. What's this about?"

"Your brother's dead," Katie answered. "Let's go, Melanie. We're ending this now." She stormed off. Melanie, still crying, shuffled behind her.

"Matt?" was all Liz was able to get out before Jenny cut her off.

"What's going on? Is this about my sister?"

"Yeah."

"Well?" Jenny asked, then waited.

I sighed, then answered my client. "Looks like Melanie pulled the trigger, but someone else put her up to it."

"Was it Kevin?" Jenny asked.

"Katie seems to think so."

Jenny's mouth puckered like she had just eaten a bag full of sour candy. Without saying a word, she turned and sprinted down the hall in the same direction that Katie and Melanie had gone.

I looked over at Mac. He was writing furiously. Liz still looked like she had walked in on the middle of a movie that was in a language she didn't understand. "Matt?" she said.

"Yeah?"

"Do you owe me an apology?"

"Looks that way. You want it now?"

"Do we have time?"

"Depends on how much you like your brother."

"What do you mean?"

"He's about to get sandbagged," I said. "You might want to be there to pick him up."

"Did he do it?" she asked.

"Depends on who you ask. We might as well get his version of the story."

All three of us headed toward Kevin's locker. We didn't run, but we sure as hell didn't take the scenic route.

23

As Liz, Mac, and I were speed walking to Kevin's locker, the bell rang. Kids poured into the hallway from all directions, like water into a sinking ship. We slowed down to a crawl. By the time we got there, Katie was already chewing on Kevin's hide. Melanie stood nearby, like a little girl watching her parents fight. Jenny looked like she wasn't sure who to hate yet.

"I don't know what the hell you're talking about," Kevin said.

"Bull! You knew my sister had a crush on you, and you used it to get what you wanted!" Katie poked Kevin's chest with every "you." "You were scared of Nikki, so you let a little girl do your dirty work!"

"You're out of your mi—"

Katie cut him off with a swift right to the gut. Kevin went down to his knees, palms to the floor, like an obedient dog. Kids watched intently to see what was going on, but kept their distance.

"Big man," Katie sneered at him, "taking advantage of a little girl. Well, how about this little girl?" she asked, pointing her thumbs at herself. "You want to try that stuff with me?"

"The craziest part of this," Kevin coughed out, "is that you think you're little."

She almost kicked him in the stomach. She seemed to have forgotten that she was in a hallway full of witnesses. I reminded her.

"Maybe you should keep your nose out of hall monitor business, Stevens."

"That doesn't look like business to me. That looks like pleasure," I said. "And I'm sure there's a couple of kids in this hallway who would agree with me."

Katie looked around, her foot still cocked and ready. She quickly came to the realization that she was the center of attention, and kicking a kid when he was down might not be good for her permanent record. She lowered her foot, but you could tell she wasn't happy about it.

"Thanks for setting a good example," I said, "for the children."

She gave me a response that was half grunt, half growl, then grabbed Kevin's left arm and twisted it behind his back. He winced, but didn't make a sound. He didn't want to give her the satisfaction.

"You're hurting him!" Liz yelled, but Katie didn't seem to hear her. She brought Kevin to his feet in what looked like the most painful way possible.

"Let's go, scumbag," Katie said, and started to lead him off.

Jenny stepped in front of them. She took her time and made a show of it, shaking with fury, looking up at him with disgust, and finally rearing back and slapping him across the face. Kevin's head barely moved. "That's for my sister," she said. She lifted her notebook and was about to beat Kevin with it when Katie started moving.

"Okay. You got your free shot," Katie said, "now get out of the way." She shoved Jenny aside and led Kevin down the hall. Liz followed close behind, making sure Katie didn't take any more cheap shots along the way.

Melanie tried to sneak out, hoping that she had been forgotten in the melee, but her sneaker squeaked loudly on the polished floor tile. Her luck, if she had any to begin with, had officially run out. Jenny grabbed her arm and spun her around. "You little witch! You were my friend! How could you!" Jenny reared back to hit her, but she wasn't fast enough. Melanie squirmed out of her grip and did the only thing she knew to do in a crisis: She ran after her sister.

Jenny ran two steps after her, but I grabbed her before she could get any farther. "Let go of me!" she screamed, and struggled to break free.

"You're in no shape for a hallway chase."

"Let go of me!"

"Too late," I said. "Melanie's long gone."

"Great. Are you happy?"

"Calm down, Jenny. This is middle school. It's not like she hopped a plane to Mexico."

She started to walk off.

"Where are you going?" I asked.

"Take a wild guess."

"Don't do it."

"What should I do instead? Huh, Matt? Just let them get away with a slap on the wrist?"

"Katie doesn't slap wrists. She knocks heads."

"I want more."

"I see. What happened to all that talk about wanting justice, not revenge?"

"You were right all along, Matt. Justice isn't enough."

"So, you think getting an eye for an eye will make you feel better? Putting them in the Outs won't solve anything."

"That's the difference between you and me, Matt. I don't want to solve anything. I just want them to hurt."

"Spoken like Nikki Fingers's little sister."

Jenny didn't look at me. She just reached into her pocket and pulled out a crumpled pile of dollar bills. She stuffed them into my hand. "Here," she said, "you earned it. Thanks for everything. You're fired."

"I'm not going to let you take them out," I said.

"It isn't up to you."

"It could be."

"Matt," she said, a small, angry smile on her face. She leaned in and kissed me lightly on the cheek. When she pulled away, it was clear that the innocent, little Jenny was gone. The true heir to Nikki Fingers was in her place. "Don't get in my way. This is the only warning you'll get." She turned and walked off before I could respond, her ponytail swishing side to side in a way that used to make me happy. Her crumpled ones sat in my hand like used tissues.

"Jenny always *seemed* innocent, but she was really the fiercer of the two," Vinny said, appearing behind me.

"Not Nikki?"

"You'd think so, but no. Nikki was more . . . calculating." Vinny looked over at Jimmy Mac. "Shouldn't you go cover the story?" There was nothing gentle about his suggestion. Mac didn't say anything, but he almost sprained his neck in agreement. He practically left skid marks on the tile.

Vinny waited until Mac was gone before he spoke.

"Are you going to try to stop her?"

"Jenny? I was thinking about it."

"Don't think too long, if you expect to have any chance."

"Sounds like you speak from experience."

He smiled and nodded. "She's given me a bit of trouble in the past."

"You don't seem to mind that much," I said.

He shrugged as if that were an answer. "It's too bad it had to come to this," he said. "I just wish I had seen it coming."

"Well, you've got a lot going on."

"Well . . . ," he said, missing my sarcasm, or pretending to, "congratulations on solving the case."

"You're sure about that?"

"Of course. It makes perfect sense. Kevin had the means and the motive. He was crushed when Nicole left him behind."

"So he put her in the Outs?"

"Kids have done worse for less reason. Maybe he thought there was someone else."

"Was there?"

"I wouldn't know." He started walking away. "Listen, forget all this. It's over. You solved it. Come by my table at lunch today and pick up the rest of your fee, plus a nice bonus."

"Right."

He stepped back toward me. "Really great job, Matt. Really great." Before he walked off, he clapped me twice on the shoulder. I had no idea why, but I suddenly felt like a boxer who was being paid to take a fall, and Vinny's clap on the shoulder felt like the weak punch that was supposed to knock me out.

24

I walked to my locker with Kevin's love notes still in my hand. Katie was going to want them for evidence, but for now they were mine. They seemed to be the final piece of the puzzle, filling in the backstory for Melanie and Kevin's crime. Yet something was still bugging me, like a piece of meat stuck between my back teeth. I sat on the floor next to my locker to take another look.

All the same phrases from before jumped out at me. "Do it and we'll be together." "Nikki is the only thing standing in our way." I started from the beginning, reading this time instead of skimming.

It was in the second note, halfway down the first page: "I remember it like it was yesterday," it read. "I was sitting in my fifth-grade class. You walked by, just as Mrs. Esposito was rambling on in her nasally voice about the Declaration of Independence. I couldn't take my eyes off of you."

I reread the sentence. It said the same thing the second time around. I pulled out the forged hall pass from my back pocket, a realization hitting me like a blind cyclist. I held the signature by "Mr. Allan" next to the sentence I had just read. The handwriting looked different enough, unless you looked closely. The double "L's" in "nasally" and "Mr. Allan" stood out like water in the desert.

There was one more connection I didn't want to make, but I had to. I pulled out a note that had been left in my locker just a few days ago. I knew before looking that they would be there. The double "L's," upright and balloony, like no other "L's" I'd seen. The connections were suddenly obvious. I hustled over to Katie's office, hoping I wasn't too late. Someone deserved Jenny's brand of justice. It just wasn't Kevin.

Liz was waiting dutifully outside Katie's door. Jimmy Mac was crouched beside a row of lockers, trying to make himself invisible. His pen was poised, waiting for something to happen. When I approached, they both opened their mouths to speak. I put my index finger to my lips, silently telling them to be quiet. They snapped their mouths shut.

I glanced at the clock on the wall. I had to be quick. Only eight minutes 'til the bell rang.

"Jenny?" I said.

"I don't think she's—" Liz started to say before I shushed her.

"Jenny?" I scanned the hallway, looking for possible places to hide. There were only a couple hundred. I prowled around as if I were in a minefield. Liz and Jimmy Mac watched me nervously. "I know you're around," I called out. "I can hear your angry breathing."

"Don't strain your eyes, Matt," Jenny said, from around the corner. She deliberately pumped her soaker, letting me know that a head-on charge wouldn't be in my best interest. She still planned to take Kevin and Melanie out, just as soon as they left Katie's office.

"Don't do this, Jenny," Liz said. "Please."

"I'm sorry it has to be this way. But they took out my sister!"

"I know," Liz said, as if she were admitting something

she never wanted to face. “Kevin’s not a good guy, but he’s my brother and I love him, so please don’t do this!”

“Nikki’s my sister! He took her out! What do you expect me to do?”

The door to Katie’s office opened, interrupting this battle of the dutiful sisters. Liz’s eyes went wide as she froze in place, not sure what to do. I still couldn’t see Jenny, but I could feel her tense up, ready to pounce and spray anything that moved.

“Katie!” I yelled. “Don’t come out!”

“No!” Jenny screamed like a wounded animal. She popped out of her hiding spot, her Super Soaker poised and ready.

Katie’s door stopped in mid-swing. “What the hell’s going on out there?”

“Nothing!” Jenny shouted. “Come on out!”

“We’ve got a little situation out here,” I said. It was a mild understatement. “You’re better off right now listening from behind that door.”

“Shut up, Matt!” Jenny pointed her squirt gun at me. “They have to get what’s coming to them! They deserve it!”

“No, they don’t. If anyone deserves it, Jenny, it’s you.”

"What?"

Liz looked at me, the realization creeping across her face. "Matt, you mean . . . ?"

"Yeah. Jenny's behind this whole thing."

Everything stopped. Then Jenny started laughing.

"You're crazy," she said through her giggles.

"You're the one who wrote these love notes to Melanie, not Kevin. You forged his handwriting."

"You're making this up, Matt. To spare your precious girlfriend's brother. I'm not going to be your patsy!"

"You don't have to be. You're guilty."

"Why would I take out my own sister? Huh?"

"The same reason most people do anything," I said. "Money. You and Vinny had a great little forgery operation set up, and Nicole was going to make you take it down."

"No. I just met Vinny the other day."

"You two should get your stories straight. He says he's known you for years."

"He's lying, and even if he isn't, what does that prove?"

"Nothing on its own. Plenty when you combine it with these." I held up "Kevin's" notes. "You made one fatal mistake. You had 'Kevin' write, 'I was sitting in my fifth-grade class. You walked by, just as Mrs. Esposito was rambling on in her nasally voice about the Declaration of Independence.'"

"So?"

"Kevin didn't have Mrs. Esposito in fifth grade. He sat next to me, in Mr. Green's class."

"So what?" Jenny said, laughing. She was getting nervous, twitchy, and she still had the squirt gun pointed at me.

"The notes don't stand up, Jenny. They work on the quick glance, but not on the long look. Even an amateur can see that, and Katie's no amateur." I held one of the forged passes up to the note that Jenny had written to me, the one that told me to "call" her, the one she wrote on Wednesday. What felt like a million years ago. "You never got your 'L's down, especially the doubles.

"Nikki had left Vinny's crew and a life she loved to try to be a good example to you," I said. "She had no idea that you and Vinny had been in business right from the start. But she found out and she wasn't happy. She was going to shut you down, and you weren't strong enough to stop her."

Jenny didn't say anything. Her eyes darted back and

forth. She was trying to decide who to take out first. I kept talking, trying to keep her occupied.

"You had to take her out, but didn't think you could do it on your own. You thought of a plan. You knew that Joey Renoni had a crush on Melanie, but Melanie loved Kevin and would do anything for him. It was easy to get to her. All you had to do was forge some letters—not a problem with all the free samples that Kevin wrote to your sister. You dangled a promise of Kevin's love in front of Melanie's face, and provided her with the means and the plan to take out Nikki."

She started laughing. "Matt, this is ridiculous! Why would I do it, then hire you to find me?"

"You didn't hire me to find you. You hired me to find Melanie and Kevin. You thought you had it all sewn up. You were friends with Melanie, so you knew exactly which buttons to push to make her believe that Kevin really wanted her. You knew that Katie hated Kevin because Melanie was in love with him. And you knew that whatever you pinned on Kevin was going to stick, because Katie would want it to, especially when she saw the notes."

"Matt," Jenny said sweetly, still holding the gun on

me, "you don't really believe this, do you? I saved you from that booby trap in your locker."

"A booby trap that you set. It was a win-win situation for you. If you saved me, I'd never suspect you were behind it. If you didn't, then I was out of the picture, and maybe the case would never get solved. Either way, you were okay with the outcome."

"Matt, I would never try to hurt you," she said in a way that was supposed to make me drop what I was doing and grovel at her feet.

"Sorry, kid, that might have worked on Tuesday, but I'm a little older now, and a whole lot wiser."

Her smiled faltered. "You're a little light on proof, don't you think?"

"Well, there is one thing," I said. "After you set the booby trap in my locker, you found something and took it. You knew you probably shouldn't have, but you couldn't help yourself. It was your sister's, and because you took her out, you believed it was yours now. You have it on you right now, you're too proud not to. I don't think it has any good luck left, though. I think your sister used it all up."

For a moment, Jenny just stood there, as if she was trying to decide whether the charade was worth keeping up. Finally, she pulled the little surfer girl figurine out of her pocket. A wicked little grin spread across her face, like crude oil seeping into the ocean. "Oh, I don't know," she said, "I think it still has a little left."

"Jenny?" a small voice said from behind Katie's door. It was Melanie. "You?"

"Sorry, Mel," Jenny said, without sounding sorry at all. "You were a good friend and all, but business is business." She pumped her squirter twice for emphasis.

"You can't get all of us," I said.

"Oh, no?" she asked. She lifted up the bottom of her cardigan. Tucked in her waistband were two little squirt guns. "The soaker is for whoever's brave enough to go first. These," she said, referring to the smaller guns, "are for the cowards who are left. What do you say, Matt? Are you feeling brave today?"

"You're not fast enough," I said.

"Ha! You think Nikki was fast? I used to hide and watch her practice, seeing how she shaved time off her draw, knowing where I could make even further improvements. Never underestimate the power of sibling rivalry."

Out of the corner of my eye, I saw Liz inching toward Jenny. I stood stone still.

"Nikki was such a hypocrite," Jenny scoffed. "She was a monster, yet she thought she could tell me what to do. She wanted to put me out of business—a business that I built from the ground up, with no help from anybody! She had no problem using her talents, but wanted to stop me from using mine. Do you really think that's fair?"

Liz kept inching over to Jenny. I used every bit of willpower to not look her way.

"Of course not. But that's okay. I've got the cure for what ails me right here," Jenny said, tapping her soaker. "In two minutes, that bell's going to ring and fill this hallway with kids, kids who love to see a good show. You want to give them a good show, Matt?"

"You think you're as good as your sister?" I asked. "So did every other two-bit hood that came through this place. What makes you different?"

"Keep talking, Matt. Make me feel better about taking you out."

"You're all talk, Jenny. In the end, you didn't even take Nikki out. You had someone else do it for you, a scared and lovesick little girl. How does *that* prove you're better than your sister? Huh? To me it says you're scared of her."

"You'd better shut up."

"You're scared of her! You're never going to be half as

good as she was. You're always going to be the plain, ordinary, invisible sister to Nikki Fingers."

"Shut up!" The squirt gun was pointed straight at me now. She was pumping it furiously, building up pressure.

"You're second-rate, Jenny! Even if you do manage to take us all out, you know what everyone's going to say? There goes Nikki's little second-rate sister!"

"Shut up! Shut UP! SHUT UP!"

"AAAAAAA!" Liz yelled, and pounced. Jenny turned and pulled the trigger. The blast was like a cannon. It struck Liz dead center, right below her waist. She fell backward, about five feet away from me. She had a shocked and helpless look on her face, and a giant, spreading wet spot on her pants.

The bell rang.

Kids streamed out of the classrooms. They started drifting over, noticing that something was up. Liz closed her eyes. Her middle-school life was over before it had begun, and she only had a couple of seconds left before the laughter would start.

Jenny looked down at her in disbelief. "Liz, I—"

"AAAAAA!" Melanie came barreling out of Katie's office, her scream full of pain and rage. Jenny tried to reach the squirt guns in her belt, but she panicked and fumbled them. Melanie hit her full force, tackling her,

sending the squirt guns skidding across the tiles.

The kids in the hallway saw Melanie and Jenny fighting and swarmed around them. They weren't disappointed. Melanie and Jenny fought like wolves over a single piece of meat. It made the fight Kevin and I had the other day look like a tea party.

Nobody even noticed Liz. Before they got a chance, I grabbed her and threw her over my shoulder in a fireman's carry. I started running with no idea where I was headed. "Anyplace in particular you want to go?" I asked. "The nurse's office? The cafeteria? Kansas City?"

"Over here!" It was Katie, holding the door to the janitor's closet open. I ran inside. She shut the door behind us. The catcalls and cheers in the hallway continued, but were muffled by the thick closet door. It took me a minute, but I found the light switch and flicked it on. I reluctantly put Liz down.

"You okay?" I asked, my heart still beating in a Morse code rhythm.

"I think so. Did anyone see?"

"No. I think we made it."

Liz started crying a little. "I thought it was over for me. I thought I was in the Outs. I thought—" She cried a little harder.

"Sssshhh." I pulled her close. She buried her head in my chest and sobbed.

"I'm sorry, Liz . . . for the accusation . . . for a lot of things."

Liz stopped crying and looked up at me. "I think you more than made up for it," she said through her sniffles. She hugged me tight again.

I don't know how long we stayed like that, but multiply it by forever and it still wouldn't have been long enough. Someone knocked on the door, ending the moment, reminding me that there were other people in the world. "Yeah?" I barked.

"It's Kevin," came the muffled voice from the other side. "Liz, hang tight. Jimmy Mac is getting you some sweatpants."

"Thanks," I called back.

"You sound different, Liz."

"This whole experience has changed me," I said.

"Yeah, hey, tell Matt to get the hell out of there and leave my sister alone," he said. He almost pulled it off without laughing.

I turned to Liz. "I should leave."

She nodded. "You're going to talk to Vinny now, aren't you?"

"He's my client."

"I'm going with you."

"With those wet pants? Not a good idea."

She rolled her eyes. "After I change."

"Still not a good idea. Listen, Chess Club, I know you're tough and all—"

She shot me a look that shut me up. "You have some things to say to him? So do I."

"You'll have to wait your turn."

"Fine. I'll be right behind you in line."

"Not today."

"Wait for me, Matt. Please. We'll go together."

"Okay," I said. "You bet." I could tell she didn't believe me. That's okay. I was lying.

I slipped out, closing the door behind me. Kevin was leaning against the wall to the right of the door, guarding it so nobody else would go in. "Matt."

"Kevin."

"Where is everybody?"

"Lunch. Didn't you hear the bell ring?"

"I guess not. That door is pretty thick."

"Mm-hmm. Right." He smiled as if he didn't quite believe me.

"What happened to the fight?"

"Katie let it go on for a while, until she was sure you got away. Then she swooped in and broke it up."

"Who won?"

"Neither of them. They're both gonna get a five-day vacation. Jenny's the only one who looks like she's been in a fight, though."

"Yeah?"

"Shiner and a fat lip. Nothing major. She deserved more."

"Katie'll see to that."

"Yeah." He paused. "Matt, thanks for . . . you know . . . "

"I didn't do it for you."

"Yeah, I know. But I benefited, so thanks."

"Okay." There was an awkward silence. "I have to go," I said finally.

"Vinny knew about this, didn't he?" Kevin asked.

"Of course he knew. What happens around here that he doesn't know about?"

"And he was going to let me take the fall."

"That's one way to look at it."

"Is there another way?"

"Not that I can tell."

Just then, Mac came running over, a pair of black sweatpants in his hand. "Hey guys. Here." He held the sweats out to Kevin. "They should fit her."

Kevin held them up and snickered. They wouldn't have fit on Kevin's arms, let alone his legs. "Good thing these are for my little sister."

"So what? I'm petite," Mac said. "If you're just gonna have a laugh at my expense, I'll take 'em back."

"No. You're right. Sorry." Kevin knocked on the door. It cracked open a couple of inches. "Special delivery." He shoved the pants in then shut the door.

"Listen," I said, "I have to go before Liz comes out."

"How come?"

"She thinks it's a good idea to come with me."

"It isn't?"

"She's already too involved in this as it is."

Kevin shrugged. "If you say so."

"You want me to come?" Mac asked.

"No thanks, Jimmy. I've got to do this alone." He looked relieved, as if his brain was angry at his mouth for making the suggestion. I started walking away. "See you around, guys."

"Hey, Matt," Kevin said. I stopped. "Be careful."

"I always am. It hasn't made a difference yet."

The cafeteria was in full lunchtime swing, but I wasn't hungry. I was there to check in with Vinny, my other client, the one who hadn't tried to shoot me with a squirt gun . . . yet. I approached his table in the back of the caf. The same two bodyguards from before blocked my path.

"Routine weapons check," the one on the right said, repeating his stock line.

"Let me guess," I said to the guard on the left, "just doing your job?"

The guard on the left froze. I had stolen his line, and now he wasn't sure what to do. "Yeah."

"You boys need a better act," I said. "This one's a little stale." I kicked the guard to my left in the shin, hard. His eyes bugged out of his head, and he gave me a little "Ah!" When he reached down to grab his shin, I grabbed his hair and pulled down. His forehead connected to my knee. His head wasn't that tough, only as hard as a cinderblock. The guard on the right lumbered toward me. He looked confused, his tongue hanging out of his open mouth, as if he had just tasted something new and unpleasant. I slapped the bottom of his chin, snapping his jaw shut, catching his tongue like a mouse in a trap. He started jumping around, yelping in pain. The kid whose shin I kicked was still hunched over, holding his forehead. I grabbed the bottom of his shirt and pulled it up and over his head, immobilizing his arms. I got behind him and gave him a healthy kick in the butt. He went flying forward and crashed into his buddy, whose hands were covering his mouth in a vain attempt to make the pain in his tongue go away. They fell to the floor in a groaning heap. "Still needs a little work," I said, "but it's an improvement."

"Impressive," Vinny said.

"Yeah?" I grabbed him by the collar and lifted him out of his seat. "Wait 'til you see act two."

He calmly raised his juice box to his mouth and took a sip. "Hello, Matthew. Here for your payment?"

"Yeah. That and more. You hung me out to dry, Vinny, and I can't say I'm happy about it."

"What do you mean?"

"Jenny was the forger and you knew it. When you found out she was responsible for the Nikki hit, you rolled over and played dumb."

"I don't know what you're talking about." Vinny took another nonchalant sip from his juice box. I knocked it out of his hands. It hit the wall with a dull thump, leaving a purple blotch that looked like modern art.

"I guess I'm not thirsty," he said.

"There was no downside for you. If I fell for the Kevin/Melanie story, Jenny stayed in the background, Kevin got one more black mark on his record, and you'd get to have a nice laugh at the Kondos' expense. If I uncovered the truth, Jenny would become notorious, your new Nikki Fingers. Maybe she's not as skilled with the squirter, but she's pretty damn good with a pen."

"So many scenarios," he said, "all unsubstantiated."

"All you had to do was give up on Nikki. She was

already out of your organization, so you didn't care. You had no use for her anymore anyway, right?"

The playful light went out of his eyes. "I'll always care about Nikki. Jenny's guilty, not me."

"Oh, so when she comes back from suspension, you're going to put her in the Outs, right?"

"I've never put anyone in the Outs."

"No, of course not. Especially when they've got a skill you find useful."

"Careful, Matthew," he said.

"Why? You keep saying you're harmless. Why should I be careful?"

"You're right," he said, a malevolent smile spreading across his face. "You shouldn't be careful at all."

"What happened to you?" I asked, ignoring his threat. "What happened to the kid who knew what it was like to get picked on?"

Vinny's smile disappeared. "Oh, he's still here."

"Bull. All I see is a former doormat who's obsessed with power. Loyalty and honor are only words you throw around in order to get other kids to do what you want. When you're finished with them, you throw them to the curb, like so much garbage."

I had pushed the right button. His face flushed red, his eyes bulged out, and I thought steam was going to come out of his ears. "You don't know anything about me," he said through gritted teeth.

"I know enough to make me si—"

Two strong hands came out of nowhere and yanked me off of Vinny. It was Brian, Vinny's former and disgraced bodyguard, the kid the size of Australia, the kid looking to get back into Vinny's good graces. He held me off the floor as if I were weightless. "Ask Brian here about my loyalty," Vinny said as he straightened out his rumpled collar. "Although I suspect he already gave you his answer." Vinny put his face an inch from mine, grabbing my cheeks so my mouth puckered. "You know nothing about me," he growled. "Nothing. But I'm going to teach you." He let go of my face, reached into his pocket and pulled out twenty dollars. He put the bill in my shirt pocket. "Lesson number one: I always pay my debts, monetary or otherwise. Are you keeping up with me?"

"You mind starting over? I wasn't listening."

Vinny didn't smile, but he did nod. Brian punched me in the stomach. I would have crumpled to the floor, but

Brian was kind enough to hold me up. "Lesson number two—"

"Always watch your back," someone said behind Brian. Suddenly, Brian's grip on me loosened. My feet hit the floor, followed closely by my butt. Liz ran over to me.

"Matt, are you okay?"

I held my stomach, which had taken its fair share of abuse over the past week. I nodded yes instead of saying it, afraid that if I opened my mouth I'd hurl. I turned to see Brian wincing, someone's hand pinching the nerve in his shoulder.

"Kevin?" Vinny asked.

"Hey, Vin," Kevin said, poking his head out from behind Brian's enormous body, his hand still clamped on the nerve. "I have a couple of things I have to discuss with you, after Matt, of course."

"Matt and I were just finishing up," Vinny said.

"Yeah, it looked that way."

"Gah . . . ," Brian squawked, his body twisting in pain

"Oh, I'm sorry Brian. Was I hurting you?" Kevin let go of the nerve. Brian finally exhaled. He held his aching shoulder as if it were going to fall off.

I looked around. Kevin had a lazy smile on his face.

Vinny looked like he could've been in someone's garden, discussing the weather. Liz and I seemed to be the only ones who noticed that we were surrounded by Vinny's guards. All of them were holding soakers at the ready, but they looked unsure. There was something going on between Kevin and Vinny, something that might explode at any moment. But the guards had spent as much time protecting Kevin as they had Vinny, and if things escalated between them, nobody had any idea what to do.

"So, what were you two talking about, Matt?" Kevin asked.

"Not much. You know, this and that. The whole Jenny business."

"Right, right. Did you hear, Vinny? Somehow I got accused of the whole thing."

"You're kidding."

"No. Do you believe it?" Kevin's eyes were firmly locked onto Vinny's. Neither one of them blinked. My eyes dried out just looking at them. "Matt here figured the whole thing out. Cleared me. I guess I owe him a little."

"No, you owe me a lot."

Kevin chuckled. "All right, I'll give you that one.

Vinny, Matt mentioned that you might have known a little something about the setup. I tried to tell him no, that you would never do that to someone who knows so much about the inner workings of your . . . what are we calling it this week? An organization?"

Vinny didn't answer.

"Sure," Kevin continued, "let's call it that. I told Matt that I know so much about how this organization runs, that even if Vinny didn't pride himself on his loyalty, he'd be crazy to hang me out to dry like that."

"You're right," Vinny said.

"I know. That's what I told Matt. But, he said he wanted to ask you anyway. 'No harm in asking,' he said." His and Vinny's eyes were still locked. "Was there, Matt?'

"Was there what?"

"Any harm in asking."

"Little bit."

"Yeah. Kinda knew there would be. Did you get any answers?"

"Not really," I said. "He didn't admit it, but he didn't deny it either. Said my accusations were 'unsubstantiated.'"

"Wow. Big word."

"I know," I said. "That's high school vocabulary."

"Did he say anything else?" Kevin asked.

"Nope. Just gave me a sly little smile."

"Hmm. Well, that's not really an admission of anything."

"I know. He's pretty slippery."

"Still," Kevin said, "I find it hard to believe that he didn't know anything."

"You're right. Hard to believe."

"What do you say, Vinny?" Kevin asked. "Did you know anything? Tell the truth."

For a second, I didn't think Vinny was going to answer. I thought they were going to stay frozen like that, eyes locked, until the end of time . . . or at least until the final bell of the school day. Then Vinny blinked. It wasn't much, but in the context of what was happening, it was everything. "Nothing," Vinny said. "I knew nothing."

"Well, he seems honest. What do you think, Matt?"

"I'm not sure you want my opinion of him."

Kevin laughed. "Fair enough. Well, I guess I'm just going to have to go with my gut on this one. I'll trust you, Vinny. Because after all, what's a relationship without trust?"

Vinny knew better than to answer. "Well, that's it then," Kevin said. "You and I are fine."

"Glad to hear it," Vinny said. They shook hands, and everything appeared to be okay between them, but it was obvious that it wasn't. Their mouths were telling one story while their eyes were telling another.

"Matt and Liz," Kevin said, "would you guys mind taking off? Vinny and I have a couple of other things we need to discuss."

"I haven't gotten my turn yet," Liz growled. Her hands started to look like claws as she took a step toward Vinny. If I hadn't grabbed her, she might have given him a new nickname, like "Vinny One-Eye."

"C'mon, Liz," I said. "Let's go get some air."

"After I get my turn." Behind me, I heard the sound of several soakers being pumped. The guards had allegiance to Kevin, but that didn't extend to his sister, or to me for that matter.

"Now, Liz. One close call was enough for today."

She paused. "Fine," she said, without taking her eyes off Vinny. "We'll finish this later."

I escorted her out of the caf, and only had to drag her half the way. I took a glance back to see what we had escaped. Kevin and Vinny were talking like they hadn't missed a beat. The guards were invisible again. The lunchroom had returned to its familiar rhythm. On the surface, it appeared that everything was back to the way it was. I wasn't so sure. Something had shifted a little while ago between Kevin and Vinny, and I wasn't sure anything would be the same again.

When we got outside, Liz exploded. "I don't believe him! That son of a—"

"Whoa. Calm down. You'll blow out a barrette."

"I just want to take his arrogant, fat face and just—" Instead of using words to finish her sentence, she gritted her teeth and squeezed her fists into tight balls. If she were holding oranges, we'd have a nice glass of fresh juice.

"Why don't you hit something? It'll help get some of your—ow!" She punched me in the arm.

"You're right. I feel a little better."

"Glad I could help." I rubbed my arm. I made a mental note to never let another girl punch me again. For a boy, it was a no-win situation.

"My brother is such an idiot!" she yelled, ramping back up again. "How can he pretend like nothing happened?"

"Forget about him. Come on. Let's go for a walk." I grabbed her hand.

She looked down at my hand holding hers, then looked back up at me and smiled. I had taken her hand out of friendship, but sometime during the day we had crossed over the border of friendship and into something else. I don't think either of us knew the details of where or when; the only thing we were sure of was that it had happened. And in case my brain wasn't sure, my heart skipped a couple of beats in order to give it the message.

"Umm . . . ," I said, suddenly aware of the weight of my tongue. Somehow, this was much scarier than facing off against Vinny and his goons, or Jenny and her squirt guns. This felt like the opposite of the situations I was used to: I'd never want to talk my way out of this, but I was afraid that somehow, I would manage to.

"Let's go downtown and get a soda," Liz said.

"School's not over."

"It's Friday. Live a little." She smiled at me. I relaxed. She had a knack for making the hard stuff easy. It was something that I had always loved about her.

"You're the boss," I said.

"Damn straight."

"Hey! Where are we going?" came a voice from behind us. It was Kevin. My first reaction was to try to drop Liz's hand, but it was already too late. There was no way he didn't see it.

Liz looked at me and smiled again. She held my hand tighter. "*We,* as in Matt and I, are going to get a soda."

"Is that right?"

"Yeah. Why don't you go hang out with your 'organization' buddies and leave Matt and me alone?"

"What if I don't approve?"

Liz laughed. "It's so cute that you think that matters."

"It may not matter to you, but it'll matter to him," he said, pointing at me.

"Please," I said, finally finding my voice. "Nothing's changed. You're still too slow and clumsy to scare me."

"Yeah," Liz piped in. "Plus now, it's two against one."

"Whoa. Fine. I give up," Kevin said, raising his hands in mock surrender. "You guys are pretty tough. Any openings in your crew?"

"You couldn't handle it," I said. "Plus, you'd have to leave the one you're already in."

"Yeah. We don't allow dual membership."

Liz and I laughed. Kevin just stood there looking at us, a weird little smile on his face. Liz got there first, gasping a little when she realized what the smile meant. It took me a second, but I caught up.

"You serious?" I asked.

"Maybe," he answered.

"Looks like we have some stuff to talk about over sodas."

"Good deal." Kevin's smile was warm and full of relief. "Last one there has to pay," he said, then pushed me to the ground.

My hand slipped out of Liz's as I went down. "What the hell . . . ?"

Kevin was already off and running. "Race you!" he yelled over his shoulder.

Liz looked at me on the ground. She was laughing. "Matt. I'm sorry."

"For what?"

"For this." She took off running.

"Hey!" I sprang up and ran after them, smiling and

laughing the entire time. For the first time in a while, I felt like a kid again. The whole weekend stretched out in front of me like a forest full of trails, each leading someplace wild and uncharted, but full of promise. Everything seemed possible on a Friday, twenty dollars in my pocket, and the early afternoon sun warming my face as I raced my friends to see who was buying.

ACKNOWLEDGMENTS

So many people contributed to this book getting written that it's hard to narrow it down to the few who will fit here (and prevent it from sounding like an '80s power ballad) . . . but I'll give it a shot . . .

Thanks to my agent, the amazing Stephen Barbara, whose patience, instincts, and insight has been invaluable. To my editor, the fantastic Susan Van Metre, who "got it" from the get-go. Her enthusiasm, deft touch, and spot-on notes made this story hum. When she liked it, I knew it was right. I'd also like to thank Howard, Jason, Chad, Scott, Nathan, and everyone at Amulet for their hard work and boundless creativity. This has been an incredible experience because of you.

To my mom, dad, and sister, Laura, for their honest notes and constant love and support. I wouldn't be here without you. To my big Italian family (Nonnie!!), who never thought I was crazy for wanting to write and always accepted me for who I am. (Grandma, Grandpa, and Pop . . . I miss you . . .) And to Frances, Garret, and the rest of my family on the West Coast, thank you for always believing in me.

To my friends Melissa and Peter, Steve and Sarah, Will and Sara, Joe, John and Melannie, Aya, Regan, Johannah and Anthony, Mark, and Dr. Cole, whose belief in me never wavered, even when my belief in myself did.

To my daughter Emily, whose birth scared me into finishing the book, and whose smile and personality helped me get through some of the rough days. And finally to my wife, Teryse: If I tried to write down every way in which you supported me, I'd need a whole other book. Love ya, T . . .

About the Author

Jack D. Ferraiolo grew up in southern Connecticut and still considers middle school to be the toughest time of his life. He currently lives in northern Massachusetts with his wife, Teryse, and daughter, Emily. He has been writing and editing for television animation for close to ten years. He developed, and writes for, *WordGirl* on PBS, for which he received an Emmy nomination. *The Big Splash* is his first novel. Find out more about Jack at www.jackferraiolo.com and www.bigsplashbook.com.

THIS BOOK WAS ART DIRECTED and designed by Chad W. Beckerman. The text is set in 12-point Adobe Garamond, a typeface based on those created in the sixteenth century by Claude Garamond. Garamond modeled his typefaces on ones created by Venetian printers at the end of the fifteenth century. The modern version used in this book was designed by Robert Slimbach, who studied Garamond's historic typefaces at the Plantin-Moretus Museum in Antwerp, Belgium.